CONNEMARA DAYS

Steve Mayhew

Published by:
Red River Computing Ltd.

© 2016 Steve Mayhew (text)

The rights of Steve Mayhew as author of this work has been asserted by him in accordance with the Copyright, Designs and patents Act, 1993.

All rights reserved. No part of this publication may be reproduced, stored in a retrieval system, or transmitted in any form or by any other means, electronic, mechanical, photocopying, recording or otherwise, without the prior permission of the author and the publisher.

ACKNOWLEDGEMENTS

Grateful acknowledgement is made to the following for permission to reprint copyrighted material:

GALWAY BAY © 1947 Box & Cox (Publications) used by permission.

WILD COLONIAL BOY © 1950 Walton's Piano & Musical Instrument Galleries (Publication Dept) Ltd. Published by Box & Cox (Publications) Ltd. used by permission.

For Marilyn

If you travel west to Galway and climb the wondrous hills
That look down upon the shining loughs and bays
In years to come you will remember
When it's colder than December
Of those warm and gentle Connemara Days.

For it's in the heat of summer when clouds are banished from the sky
And the mountains wave and shimmer in the haze
That your thoughts will always wander
To a time when life was slow
And they were never-ending Connemara Days.

Anon

PROLOGUE
1992

For a moment, Thomas O'Dea was oblivious to the stark beauty of the Connemara countryside, deep in thought as he drove towards the village of Cong to attend his mother's funeral.

He traversed the lonely mountain roads that wound past Lough Corrib. The rolling peaks and valleys he had roamed as a young boy over forty years before towered to one side, while the streams to his right danced and flowed like ribbons of quicksilver in the morning sun.

Catching sight of his receding hairline in the rear-view mirror he grimaced, contemplating the passage of time. Age, however, had yet to fully deplete the shock of copper red hair that once crowned his head.

Driving past a small stone bridge spanning the stream next to the road Thomas looked in the side mirror and glimpsed two figures sitting on top of a horse-drawn cart. Stopping the car, he looked back in surprise to see the figures had disappeared.

As he surveyed the bridge where John Wayne and Barry Fitzgerald had stopped on their way to `Innisfree' in the film *The Quiet Man* many years before, Thomas came to a sudden realisation. The interminable feeling of grief that had overwhelmed him for the last few days had finally been breached by a fleeting memory of long ago. A memory that had banished, however briefly, all thoughts of his deceased mother.

Thomas looked over the waters of Lough Corrib, stretching for miles into the distance before meeting the pale bright blue of the sky. His gaze focused upon a small fishing boat that appeared to float in the sky like a tiny bird as it moved towards the horizon.

He was transfixed by the almost inert movement of the boat as it moved like a small toy on a pond. A slight breeze then blew across the lake, breaking the spell. As Thomas started up the car, he found himself thinking about the figures that had vanished on the bridge, and the boat that still seemed to float in the sky. One was an illusion of memory, the other of the light, but neither of them real. He took consolation from the fact that at least the first could be seen over and over again if one wished, something for which Thomas was thankful.

Driving down the quiet main road of Cong towards the church at the bottom of the hill, Thomas passed a shop with a sign painted above it proclaiming *Pat Cohan's Bar*. His mind instantly recalled the scene in which Victor McLaglen's stand-in flew through the shattered wooden door of the pub onto the pavement, the powerful imagery of the film breaking the bounds of his consciousness once more.

Following the road round into the car park he stopped opposite the Catholic Church and got out of the car. A bell started to ring on cue, as if to welcome him back to the village. Thomas retrieved a dark suit jacket from the back seat, straightened his tie and ran his hands through his thin hair. He then walked towards the church, the mournful sound of the organ reflecting everything he felt about the service he was about to attend.

He walked from the sunlight into the cold embrace of the church. The organ music, by some unexplained trick of the ear, wasn't as loud inside the building as it had appeared to be outside. A large wooden coffin rested on a trestle in front of the altar. A sudden wave of grief momentarily pounded at his chest as he realised his mother lay inside the coffin. As Thomas entered the church the congregation of around fifteen people turned as one to catch a glimpse of the new arrival. Despite her now frail countenance and the bountiful grey hair, he immediately recognised his sister Heather, sat with her husband Joe in the front pew.

Heather smiled sweetly and waved her hand to indicate that he should join them. Thomas shuffled along the seat and sat next to Heather, nodding at Joe who smiled back at him in return.

The organ music abruptly ceased. A priest appeared, a young man in his late twenties with a freshly scrubbed face that brightened the dark corners of the church. He made the sign of the cross over the coffin then climbed the stairs to the podium. Peering down at the mourners from a lofty height he began the eulogy, his strong voice echoing out across the cavernous interior.

"This woman was a good woman, well known to everybody in the village of Cong for many years, yet no one shall know her better than God."

Heather wiped away a tear. Thomas sat with head bowed, the voice of the priest playing in the background as he slowly looked up and contemplated the wooden structure that held his mother's body.

A small crowd gathered around the open plot as the coffin was lowered into the ground. At the head of the grave lay a large pile of flowers and wreaths, and a small granite headstone rested against a tree a few feet away, ready to be put into place. Inscribed upon the stone were the words

Mary O'Dea 1912-1992
Beloved mother of Heather and Thomas
Gone to a Better World

Mary's grave had been placed close to that of her husband, his headstone bearing the simple legend

Patrick O'Dea 1908-1980

Thomas and his sister each took a handful of dirt and threw it onto the top of their mother's coffin. Heather dropped a single rose into the grave, then started to weep. Thomas put his arm around her shoulder as Joe whispered words of consolation.

The men stood either side of Heather as they joined hands and slowly made their way out of the church grounds towards a small bridge that crossed the River Cong.

Rose Cottage stood at the end of the bridge and was covered in bright summer blooms, the occasional brick peeking out from beneath the flowers and vines that enfolded the beautiful little building. Thomas gazed down into the clear waters of the stream below.

His sister and her husband joined him a moment later, the three of them pleased to be together again, brother and sister united in their common grief at the death of their mother. Their shared memories travelled back to a hot summer day many years before when the world was younger and brighter and life poured forth the promise of endless youth.

The years fell away as Heather remembered meeting Joe for the first time while Joe relived the joy of finally summoning up the nerve to approach the beautiful young woman he grew to love. Thomas smiled to himself as he recalled standing on the bridge in the very same spot more years ago than he cared to remember, his memories returning to a long hot day in 1951...

CHAPTER ONE
1951

Eight-year-old Thomas O'Dea and his friends Billy McNee and Michael Fitzgerald slowly pushed their way through the huge crowd of villagers gathered on the bridge behind the film crew, trying to catch a glimpse of the star of the film, their hero, John Wayne.

The director, John Ford, sat in a canvas chair to the left of the camera, chewing on his ubiquitous handkerchief, his eyes hidden by a pair of dark glasses. Thomas could see Wayne standing a few feet away by a large tree next to the stream, waiting to throw a fake punch at Victor McLaglen's stand-in, and knock him back into the water. He then saw Ford nodding very slightly at a man to his left, who raised a megaphone to his mouth.

"And - action!"

Thomas watched as the clapper loader raised the board with the words *The Quiet Man - Scene 38 - Take 1* inscribed on it, then snapped the wooden contraption shut. On cue, Wayne's fist flew towards the stand-in's head. The man threw himself back as if propelled by a hammer straight into the stream behind him.

Thomas, Billy and Michael burst into a spontaneous cheer along with the rest of the crowd.

Ford turned and scowled at the boys.

"Cut!" he shouted.

He fixed his dark gaze on the nervous, gangly figure of young Joe Yates, his third assistant director. "When I say I want quiet on my set, Mr Yates, then I want QUIET! Understand?" shouted Ford.

"Yes, sir," replied a querulous Joe. "Quiet it is."

Joe walked over towards the crowd.

"Come on, you guys, please, you heard the man. Let's have a little quiet over here, huh? Please?" Joe pleaded. "We're trying to make a movie here."

Billy McNee giggled as he whispered to Thomas.

"Hey, Tommy, d'ya think they call it *The Quiet Man* 'cause everybody has to be quiet all the time? D'ya?"

Before Thomas could reply a large clammy hand attached to the arm of Mary O'Dea loomed out of the sky and fixed itself to his ear like a magnet. He cried out in pain as his mother pulled him away from his friends.

 "Ouch, ma, ouch! You're hurtin' me ear!"

Mary let him go and leaned down, pointing her finger in Thomas's face for emphasis as she berated him in a loud voice. "I'll hurt more than your ear-hole before I'm through with you, my boy," she warned, twisting his half mangled ear once more for emphasis. "How many times have I told you to stay away from these people? Now. Get home with you. Your tea's been on the table for the last half an hour."

Thomas rubbed his sore ear and shut his eyes against the pain. Mary turned her attention towards his frightened companions.

"You, Billy McNee and you, Michael Fitzgerald, get home with you before your mother's start wondering what you're up to as well. Go on now, be off."

Billy and Michael fled for their lives as Mary shook her head in exasperation. "I wish your father were here right now. He'd soon sort you out."

Thomas flinched at the mention of his absent parent. Patrick O'Dea had left his family and the village of Cong nearly two years before, and had not been seen since. Even after all this time the subject of his disappearance still monopolised bar room conversation in every pub in the village. Why did he leave so suddenly?

All Thomas knew was his father would one day return, of that he was sure. As for why he had left, the answer to that question stood right in front of him, her finger so close to his nose Thomas thought he was about to go cross-eyed as well as deaf in one ear.

She wasn't a bad mother, as mothers went, he supposed. Thomas just wished she were somebody else's. That there was somebody else for Mary to direct all her exasperation and frustration with her lot in life at, other than him and his elder sister, Heather.

"Jeez, lady, will you please be quiet?" Joe shouted.

A fearful silence fell upon those gathered upon the bridge as his mother glared at Joe. It was a look so cold and focused people might wonder aloud if the other two Gorgon sisters might not be located nearby. Fortunately for Joe he had turned away seconds before and was thus spared the indignity of being turned to stone in front of a non-paying crowd. Unfortunately for Joe, however, this respite was not to last.

"Don't you be telling me when I can and cannot talk in my own village!" screamed Mary. "And don't you be blaspheming the name of Holy Jesus either or I'll be over there to clip your ears, you gawky ill-mannered little twerp!"

Ford stood with his hands on his hips, a mile-wide grin plastered across his face as Joe felt the lash of Mary O'Dea's fiery tongue. Thomas's mother pushed him in front of her as she marched away from the bridge through the silent crowd. He felt the eyes of the entire villager and the film crew staying on them until they were around the corner, at which point both of them walked straight into the path of the local Garda officer, PC Flanagan. A couple of years older than Mary's husband but ten times more reliable, Flanagan's six foot two frame of a body was supported by the largest pair of feet seen on anyone north of the Connemara border for many a year. And it was obvious to any passer-by that the tall yet thin-framed PC was very happy to see Thomas' mother.

"Good day to you, Mary," said Flanagan, tipping his hat slightly to her. Mary automatically curtsied in the face of authority, looking to the ground in order to hide the girlish delight she felt in meeting a man who was prepared to treat her with a rare display of courtesy. Flanagan rumpled Thomas' hair.

"And what's the young rascal been up to now, a?" An unimpressed Thomas shrugged Flanagan's hand away and leant against the wall a few feet further on along the street. "Oh, he's fine," lied Mary in a meek voice, avoiding eye contact with the tall PC in front of her. "Just late for his tea as usual". Flanagan smiled in return.

"So, Mary. Have you seen Patrick at all recently?" Mary silently shook her head in response to Flanagan's unexpected query.

"How he could leave the likes of you to bring up two children on his own is beyond me, it truly is". Mary kept her head lowered in shame and murmured a faintly heard 'goodbye' to Flanagan before she caught up with Thomas, jostling him along even more speedily than before in order to maintain as much distance as possible between herself and Flanagan. The officer watched as Mary hurried down the road, sighing with regret as she and Thomas disappeared around the corner.

Joe watched as John Wayne lit a cigarette and leaned against the tree next to the stream, while McLaglen's wet stand-in dried himself down with a small towel. Joe sighed with relief and was just about to issue instructions to the crowd still milling around on the bridge when Ford broke the silence.

"That's a print. Let's call it a day."

"But..." said Joe, confused that they had only done one take.

"But what, Mr Yates?" asked Ford in a calm voice.

Wayne gave Joe a pitying look, a look that said to Joe that Wayne knew only too well what the young man was about to go through.

"I... I just... well, I thought maybe..." stuttered Joe. Even the extras were now taking notice.

"You thought maybe what?" prodded Ford.

Joe glanced around at Wayne, McLaglen and the rest of the crew, pleading with his eyes for somebody to intervene before Ford finished him off. But nobody had the courage to interfere.

Joe swallowed hard.

"I thought we were going for another take, Mr. Ford. Sir," he added, hoping this last touch of overbearing servility might be enough to humour the old man. He was wrong. Ford indicated the canvas chair with a jerk of his head.

"See that chair, Mr. Yates?"

Joe nodded, his eyes fixed on a small pebble on the ground two feet away. He could feel his ears and cheeks turning bright red.

"Then look at it, Mr. Yates, if you please," said Ford. Joe stared hard at the back of Ford's chair.

"Does it say *Joe Yates* on the back of my director's chair?"

Joe shook his head and returned to staring at the pebble on the ground.

"Does it, Mr. Yates?" shouted the director, all pretence of conviviality thrown to the four winds.

"No, sir."

"*No, sir* is right. It does not say *Joe Yates*, it says *John Ford*. And in the unlikely event that it might one day actually say *Joe Yates*... Well that, sonny, is the day you can go for another take."

Ford stalked off across the bridge back towards Ashford Castle where he and most of the cast and crew were billeted for the duration of their stay. Joe's humiliation burnt deep. He had prided himself on not having fallen foul of Ford's acid tongue since having been hired to work with the crew almost a month ago.

A three-time Academy Award winner for *The Informer*, *The Grapes Of Wrath* and *How Green Was My Valley*, John Ford was one of the most respected and revered of all Hollywood directors. His surly and abrupt manner coupled with a penchant for cutting down to size, in front of the whole cast and crew, those foolish enough to question his authority made him one of the most feared directors as well.

Although it was inevitable that sooner or later Ford was going to turn on him just as he had on numerous others before, Joe had clung in vain to the hope that the circumstances surrounding his fall from grace might have been somewhat less public. Alas, it was not to be. Humbled in front of his peers he stared even harder at the ground, waiting for it to open up and swallow him whole.

Wayne flicked his half-finished cigarette into the stream, then loped towards the crest-fallen young man, patting Joe on the shoulder before making his way back to Ashford Castle.

"Don't let it get to you, Joe. He does it to me all the time."

Joe appreciated the gesture. Major Hollywood stars did not normally go out of their way to comfort members of the crew, but Wayne came across as just one of the guys, something Joe was grateful for as the humiliation of a few moments before still gnawed at his insides.

Two other members of the crew, Gene Willis and Bo Willard, joined Joe in sympathetic commiseration. They had both worked with Ford before on a number of his films, and what had happened to Joe was nothing new to either of them. Gene's world-weary countenance betrayed the ingrained cynicism of one who had worked in the movie industry for nigh-on thirty of his forty-five years.

Joe knew that Gene had seen them all come and go, Erich Von Stroheim, Joseph Lubitsch, Rex Ingram, Allan Dwan. Ford was one of the last of the great silent movie directors still working in Hollywood and, despite Gene's obvious distaste for the way in which Ford continued to bait those around him, Joe was witness to the fact the Gene still couldn't hide his admiration for the way in which the old man had managed to survive in such a cut-throat business.

Joe and Gene both agreed that Ford's longevity in the industry was down to a combination of sheer bull-headedness, and an uncanny knack for knowing what the public would and would not want to see on their local cinema screens. And, ultimately, for being the best damned director ever to come out of Hollywood. Bar none.

Joe also knew, however, that Bo Willard felt John Ford to be the meanest son-of-a-bitch that ever walked God's earth. He had once told Joe that the only reason he worked with the miserable old goat was because he and Gene had started together on one of Ford's silent cowboy films, and were now both part of his stock company. The crew were guaranteed work on at least two pictures a year. After *The Quiet Man* they were all off back to the States to work on a remake of the silent First World War movie, *What Price Glory*.

The sun was sinking in the western sky somewhere over Galway Bay. The air was sweet and clean, and to top it all they had finished early. It was time for Bo, Gene, Joe and anybody else who might want to tag along to see how many of those black beers they could sink before dinner.

"We're off to Ryan's Bar," said Gene. "You coming or you gonna stand there for the rest of your life feeling sorry for yourself?"

Joe looked at his watch.

"Ryan's doesn't open for another... It's nearly five!" he exclaimed, rushing off towards the village. Gene and Bo grinned at each other.

"Hey, wait a minute. This we gotta see," said Gene with a wide grin as he and Bo hurried off after Joe.

Gallagher's Ironmongery, where Thomas's elder sister Heather had worked for the last two years, stood at the top of the hill on the main road leading out of Cong. The outside of the shop looked as though it hadn't seen a new coat of paint for a very long time, and the inside wasn't much better. Dermot Gallagher, the middle-aged proprietor, had offered Heather employment when she found herself, at the age of sixteen, having to help support her mother and Thomas after her father's unexpected departure.

She had set her heart on going to Dublin University to study Literature and the Classics, with the ambition of returning to the village and taking up a teaching post, but her father's selfish disappearing act had put paid to that. It was only through working at Gallagher's that the O'Dea's had enough money coming in to make ends meet, with Mary taking in the occasional washing and ironing jobs from the other villagers, some of whom very rarely had the money to pay in the first place.

Heather was returning from the post office after depositing the takings for the day. She turned the corner, and was nearly knocked over by her younger brother as he flew down the street towards home, their mother nipping at his heels like a sheep dog. Mary prodded her as she continued down the road.

"And don't you be dawdling either, my girl. Tea's on the table."

Heather said nothing as Mary pushed Thomas in the back, deciding it might be better to confine the daily shouting match with her mother to the house.

Back in the shop she turned the sign on the door to *Closed*, and noticed three members of the Hollywood crew loitering in a doorway on the other side of the street. In the middle of the group stood a good-looking, tall fair-haired young man, still almost a boy with his shy looks and awkward posture. Heather recognised Joe straight away. Which wasn't too difficult seeing as he had stood in the same doorway for the last two weeks practically every day watching her coming and going. It appeared that this time he had brought reinforcements. Maybe today was the day the boy might be encouraged to make his move. And maybe today was the day she helped him, she smiled to herself.

Heather could hear Gallagher whistling happily away to himself in the back room of the store.

"Heather, is that you?"

"I'll be off, Mr Gallagher. I've left the receipt from the post office by the till. See you tomorrow."

"Before you go, young lady, just come back here and take a look at all this."

Heather sighed with a tinge of frustration then hurried reluctantly to the back of the shop.

"Mr Gallagher, I'm sorry but I really…"

She stopped as she entered the small stock room to be greeted by the sight of one whole wall covered from floor to ceiling with different sized boxes. Gallagher beamed with delight as he gestured to the cardboard mountain behind him.

"Well? What do you think?" Gallagher smiled a gap-toothed smile. His rotund figure and the curly wisps of hair protruding from behind his ears always put Heather in mind of Tweedledum or Tweedledee. She could never decide which.

"What is it? What's in them?"

Gallagher could hardly contain himself as he rubbed his hands in glee. Heather thought he was so agitated he might be about to break into a little dance. A vision of Gallagher tripping merrily around the stock-room like a demented leprechaun popped into her head. She banished the unkind image before it took root and caused her to lose composure.

"Gold, Heather me dear, pure gold. They just delivered the stuff while you were away at the post office."

"I don't understand," said Heather, clearing her throat and biting her lip to keep the leprechaun at bay.

Gallagher lovingly rubbed the box nearest to him.

"In just under two weeks' time there'll be a queue outside this shop winding all the way back to the nearest village, if I'm not mistaken. People will come for miles around to beat a path to Gallagher's Ironmongers just to get a peek at these artefacts."

"Artefacts?"

"Electrical goods, Heather," he said, full of importance. "Electrical goods that I have had especially imported from the shores of …". Gallagher ripped off an invoice sheet from the top of one of the boxes, put his glasses on and read aloud.

"Made in Cincinnati, USA. Yes. Shipped all the way from America and made to me own specifications. A friend of mine

- a silent partner, shall we say - arranged the whole thing. Said I didn't have to pay those extortionate English bast... business men for their goods, when I can get them for half the price elsewhere. And this stuff has had to travel a damned sight further than just across the Irish Sea, I can tell you."

"And what kind of electrical goods might they be, Mr. Gallagher?" asked Heather, putting her jacket over her shoulders and walking from the stock room to indicate she was going home.

"Toasters, lamps, irons," replied Gallagher, following her to the door of the shop. "All we need now is the actual electricity itself to run the things on, and we'll be laughing. And, if I'm correct, it should be made available to our local community courtesy of the Electricity Supply Board in approximately..."

Gallagher made a great show of retrieving his pocket watch and gold chain from the inside of his jacket. The fact that the watch did not actually indicate the date appeared to be of little consequence to Gallagher as he proudly examined the antique timepiece with a flourish.

"Let me see now - 8 days, 4 hours and 50 minutes precisely. That would be 10pm Friday week, if I'm not mistaken." And it's just as well it is a Friday, thought Heather, knowing full well that the whole village would need the rest of the weekend to get over the celebrations.

"Actually, what is the time, Mr Gallagher?" asked Heather as she gripped the door handle.

"Just gone 5 o'clock pm precisely."

"Then I'd better be off. My mother will be wondering where I am."

She opened the door to leave.

"Where you always are," said Gallagher. "Here. Working in my shop. Like you have done for the last two years, am I right?"

"I know but you know how she frets. Ever since..." Heather left the rest unsaid. Gallagher nodded silently, smiled and held the door open for her.

"Well, you be off then. I'll see you tomorrow. Go on, I'll lock up."

As Heather left the shop she cast a surreptitious look across the road to where Joe and his friends still stood in the doorway. Joe seemed to be trying to adopt an air of nonchalance, with his long arms thrust deep into his trouser pockets, nodding his head along to a conversation with Gene and Bo.

She smiled to herself, pleased to be the object of his attention but not daring to encourage him, her bravado of a moment before deserting her in the cold light of day.

She always made a point of ensuring that once a boy took a fancy to her - and most of the boys of eligible age in the village had at one time or another made her the object of their adolescent affections - it was down to them to do all the running. Women were not born to make it easy for men. Heather's mother was certainly living proof of that.

Heather's independent state of mind had driven most of the boys in a twenty-mile radius of the village to distraction, but she had always managed to keep most of them at bay, whilst stringing them along at the same time. Her suitors had accepted this situation with good grace, mainly because there was no alternative. All of them that is except one.

Michael Cassidy.

He had no understanding of the meaning of grace as far as Heather was concerned, claiming her for his own without consent or approval. The very thought of the young farm worker with the permanently unshaven face and hands like shovels made her wince. His rudeness and aggression made it inevitable that she would have words with him one day, of that Heather was sure. But right now Cassidy was of no importance. Joe Yates occupied her thoughts entirely.

She walked down the hill certain in the knowledge that there was no need to look back. He would run after her, just like all the others. The difference this time was that Heather's curiosity was getting the better of her. Being chased was one thing. What was it like to let yourself be caught?

"Go on, Joe, go," encouraged Gene, nudging the painfully thin young man in the ribs. "Now's your chance. Quick."

"She's getting away, Joe," added Bo. "It's now or never."

Joe rushed forward then stopped. He gulped nervously and turned to his two friends.

"What do I say to her?" he asked, arms outstretched in premature defeat. Gene shook his head impatiently.

"Joe, it's not down to us to tell you what to tell her. But whatever you do, don't tell her you love her. Yet. Ask her for a date first then take it from there."

"What if she says no?" asked Joe sullenly.

"What if she says yes?" replied Bo. Joe thought about this for a second or two, scratching his head in the hope it might invoke another objection with which to defer the inevitable embarrassing confrontation with Heather.

"You think she will? Say yes, I mean?"

Gene and Bo stood with their arms folded in mock contempt at the sorry figure before them. Gene spoke in a slow staccato.

"`Joe. Go. Now. Before she disappears." He pointed to the rapidly receding figure of Heather as she made her way towards the bottom of the main street. Joe turned and hesitantly started down the hill.

"Move! Before we set the old man on ya!," shouted Gene. Still chastened from his earlier encounter with Ford, Joe sprang into life and ran across the street to catch up with Heather. "See you in Ryan's Bar," Gene called out. Joe waved to his friends as he paced down the street almost on tiptoe, clinging close to the wall should Heather suddenly turn and see him.

Heather rounded the corner at the bottom of the hill and stood outside the window of the local outfitter's shop. Ostensibly eyeing the garments on display, in reality she knew that in just a few seconds Joe would come blundering into view with all the daintiness of a herd of rogue elephants. He did not disappoint, flying round the corner and almost colliding into Heather as she stood her ground in front of the shop.

She watched as Joe leaned against the wall in an effort to disappear into the brickwork, but it was too late. Heather looked him up and down as if evaluating the worth of a piece of furniture, an extremely small, lightweight piece at that. Joe gulped and smiled as Heather stood frowning at him, hands on hips.

"I know what you're thinking but it's nothing like that at all. Honest." he said.

"What am I thinking?" said Heather, trying not to laugh while Joe continued to make friends with the wall.

"You're thinking that I'm following you, right?"

"A pretty safe assumption to make considering you've been standing outside the shop where I work for the last couple of weeks trying to get up the nerve to talk to me."

Joe's jaw dropped open in a gesture so comical Heather was barely able to keep a straight face. They stood looking at each other for what seemed an eternity. After a moment or two Heather finally shrugged and turned away.

"Same time tomorrow then," she said, starting for home once more.

"Whoa, hang on, hang on, I just... I just wanted to ask you if..."

Heather turned to face him with a cautious smile.

"Ask me what?"

She watched as Joe struggled to speak. After an agonising length of time Joe finally managed to blurt something out.

"Did you know that I'm from America?"

She knew that wasn't what he wanted to say, but Joe was clearly not in control of any of his faculties. Heather could almost feel the glowing heat from Joe's red face, but she was still obliged not to make it too easy for him.

"With an accent like that I'd never have guessed," she said.

Joe's mind and mouth suddenly came together in fractured co-ordination.

"There's a dance tomorrow night over in the village hall..."

"Yes, I know."

"...and I was wondering if maybe you might - if you're not doing anything else of course - possibly accompany me, assuming you haven't already been invited by some other person, that is, to the hall. Tomorrow. With me."

He leaned back against the wall and wiped the beads of perspiration gathered on his forehead.

"With a chaperon, of course," he added. Heather appeared to grow another foot taller as she reared up angrily.

"Chaperon?" she exclaimed. "I'm nearly twenty years of age. What would I be wanting with a chaperon? I'm perfectly capable of looking after myself. We're not all in training for the nunnery, you know."

"I'm sure you are. Capable of looking after yourself, I mean. I just meant there'd be no funny stuff, that's all." Heather had stopped playing games with Joe a long time ago.

"Why, Mr..."

"Yates, miss," said Joe, "Mr Yates. Joe..."

"Well, Mister Yates, you can take it from me that there will definitely not be any funny stuff, most certainly not with me at any rate. Tell me, Mister Yates, do you always chase people you don't know down the street then proposition them in broad daylight?" Joe shook his head vigorously.

"Oh no, miss. No. Never. Only you."

"That's good to know, Mr Yates. For a minute there I thought it might be a habit of yours. By the way, you can stop shaking your head now if you want to."

Joe stopped shaking his head. Heather turned away and started towards her house once more then stopped, calling over her shoulder to Joe.

"And what time would you be expecting to see me at this dance, if I may ask, Mr Yates?" she asked, turning back to face him.

Joe blinked, then stammered a reply

"Eight. Eight o'clock. It finishes about..." He shrugged. "...whenever, I guess."

"I'll have to be home by nine-thirty at the very latest, Mr Yates."

She brushed her hair away from her eyes, as a light evening breeze whispered through the village.

"Uh, I'm Joe."

He stuck out his hand. Heather reciprocated, both of them shaking hands awkwardly.

"I'll see you tomorrow then," said Heather. "At eight. Bye."

"Sure. Eight it is," replied Joe happily. He stood welded to the tarmac as she gave him a little wave then moved on towards her house.

Thomas threw back the door of the outside toilet and ran for his life towards the house, the Indian war party on his heels. As he burst into the house he fired a volley of shots behind him to scare the varmints away. Nobody took his scalp without a fight, he boasted to himself, blowing the smoke away from the end of his imaginary gun.

He strode down the hallway and into the kitchen. Tea was laid out on the table in the middle of the room. A meagre collection of jam sandwiches lay on a plate alongside a tin pitcher of milk. Thomas sat and grabbed a fistful of the bread, his appetite yet to recover from having been herded all the way back to the house by his mother like a stray calf. Mary stood by the sink filling up the kettle, admonishing her son at the same time.

"Have you washed your hands yet, you filthy little tyke?"

Thomas leapt up from the table and ran over to the sink, as Mary placed the kettle on the oven. Breadcrumbs trailed from the two sandwiches he had only seconds before stuffed into his mouth. He ran his hands under the tap, recoiling instinctively from the freezing water.

"This water, ma. It's really cold. When are we going to be getting the hot water, ay? When are we going to have the electricity so that we can have the hot water?"

"That's not for us, Thomas O'Dea, you mark my words. No good will come of all that new fangled electricity. Besides, it's not natural."

"Teacher says we'll be able to see properly in the streets at night," replied Thomas as he struggled with a large slab of carbolic soap. "We'll be able to stay up late and…"

"That's exactly what I mean," Mary interjected with a note of triumph. "You'll more than likely all be roaming the streets like a bunch of hooligans long after you should be in bed. Well, we're not having it in this house, that's for sure."

"Teacher says you don't have much choice. He says half the village is already set for the big switch on."

"And half the village it will stay."

"Teacher says…"

Mary angrily interrupted her son.

"Forget what teacher says. I say it will bring nothing but trouble. Just like those devils from Hollywood, taking over the village as though it's their own, pushing everybody around with their 'we want to film here' and 'move out of your house for three weeks so we can shoot there' and…"

Thomas let his mother drone on, her voice fading into the background as he gazed out of the window above the sink, just in time to see his sister coming back from work as normal. And being chased by a strange man. Which wasn't so normal.

Outside in the street Heather turned with a gasp followed by a feeling of mounting horror as she found herself staring into the face of a helplessly panting Joe Yates, both of them now not more than two feet away from the front door of her mother's house.

"I - forgot - to - ask - you - your - name," said Joe, fighting for breath.

Heather quickly glanced behind her, expecting her mother to come roaring out of the house at any minute. She backed away, shaking her head as she moved towards the front door.

"It's Heather, Heather. Go. Now. Go." Joe's heart leapt.

"Get out of here. Now!" she screeched, waving Joe away like some unwanted dog that had followed her down the street before hurrying inside. A perplexed but still eminently happy Joe whistled to himself as he made once more for Ryan's Bar.

Thomas continued to watch the silent interplay between Joe and Heather from inside the house. He dried his hands as Mary's voice returned to normal volume.

"And apart from that, I've heard somewhere all this electricity stuff gives off harmful rays that spread through the air and infect..."

Heather suddenly rushed through the door and made her towards the small hallway on the other side of the kitchen. Mary shouted out to her daughter as Heather started to hang up her coat.

"And where have you been, Miss? Gallagher's closes prompt at 5 o'clock."

Heather entered the kitchen. Her and Thomas' eyes silently met and in that instant she knew he had seen her and Joe through the kitchen window. Heather pleaded silently with him not to let on to their mother what he had witnessed. With a slight nod Thomas in turn assured her of his complete and totally unequivocal loyalty towards his sister in all matters relating to clandestine assignations with members of the opposite sex. For which of course a suitable fee would be negotiated at a later date. They sat down at the kitchen table and a relieved Heather calmly poured herself a cup of tea.

"I'm sorry I'm late, mother but I bumped into Kathy Donahue down the road," she lied, looking at Thomas in case he might be about to renege on their conspiracy of silence. She need not have worried, Thomas once more applying himself fully to the business of cramming large amounts of bread into his mouth.

"And besides, I'm eighteen years old. Surely my time is my own?"

"Not until you're twenty-one and don't you forget it. Oh, the trials and tribulations of bringing up children without a man about the house. It makes you want to weep, it really does. If only your father were here now, he'd know what to do."

"I doubt that," Heather shot back. "He was never much use to anyone when he was around anyway." Mary ignored her daughter's pointed barb as she silently sipped her tea.

Joe precariously carried three glasses of beer across the sawdust-covered floor of Michael Dunphy's pub. Gene and Bo were unable to contain themselves any longer.

"Well?" they asked in unison.

"Well what?" replied Joe as he passed the drinks around before taking his seat, his face a picture of wide-eyed innocence.

"Did she say yes?"

Joe relished the moment as he sipped his drink then slowly placed the glass on the table in front of him.

"I – I guess she did. Yeah, she said 'yes'," replied Joe with a slight tinge of incredulity. A big grin spread across his face as Gene and Bo leaned forward to hear more.

"You didn't tell her you loved her, did you?", asked a concerned Bo.

"No," Joe assured them. "But I do," he added.

Gene shook his head.

"You've got a lot to learn about women, my friend. More than we could ever teach you."

Joe attempted to divert the conversation away from the matter in hand as he looked around the pub.

"Not too busy tonight, Michael?" Joe said to the barman, who was cleaning the rim of a spotless beer glass for the third time. Dunphy was forty-five going on sixty-seven, with a barrage balloon of a stomach held in check by a huge black belt that had managed to break free from the waistband of his trousers. Breathing harshly on the glass he held it up to the fading light.

"The boys are over for a little sing-song tonight," said Dunphy. "Things may get out of hand. With a bit of luck."

At which point the door to the bar swung open and in walked the 'boys', a group of four musicians lead by Robert Quinn, a consummate flute player of indeterminate age with the fixed countenance of a professional mourner. As they passed the bar Quinn held out four fingers to Dunphy who immediately began to pour the drinks. The musicians settled themselves at the back of the pub and started tuning their instruments.

Quinn blew tunelessly on his flute as the others busied themselves respectively with a fiddle, an accordion and a washboard.

The door swung open once more to admit Vincent Corrigan, self-appointed nemesis of the Hollywood crew and general all-round pain in the neck.

Joe indicated to Gene and Bo with a nod towards Corrigan, all three of them shaking their heads at the same time in unified resignation at his unwanted presence in the bar. In his early seventies, Vincent sported a complexion to match his foul visage, his face and teeth blighted by the intake of large quantities of industrial strength poteen, manufactured in a secret illicit still.

Secret being a figure of speech rather than a fact of life. Nearly everyone living within a hundred-mile radius of Galway Bay knew or had knowledge of at least one poor soul whose health had declined drastically after having sampled the produce from Corrigan's legendary still. Which explained why nobody but Corrigan drank it anymore.

Vincent acknowledged Quinn and the musicians with a surly nod of the head, ignoring Joe and his companions not more than two feet away. He balanced on a stool in front of the bar and reached into the pocket of his threadbare coat.

"A pint please, Michael, if you will," he said.

"You're a penny short there, Corrigan," Dunphy told him as he pointed to the *6d* chalked up on the blackboard. Vincent thumped the bar in fury.

"Sixpence a pint! Are you mad? I've been drinking in this bar nearly all my life and I think it's a liberty you're taking with your patrons, Michael Dunphy. A shameful liberty. Sixpence a pint! It's illegal, that's what it is. Illegal!"

With supreme contempt Dunphy slowly turned to face the chalkboard, rubbed out the *6d* with his sleeve and chalked up *7d* instead. Vincent spluttered with indignation on the other side of the bar. One or two of the musicians tried to disguise their amusement by tuning their instruments more forcefully. Joe, Gene and Bo knew the barman was initiating the confrontation with Vincent mainly for their benefit.

Dunphy resented anybody in the village who dared to question the presence of Ford and his company in Cong. He was more than happy to capitalise upon the good fortune bestowed upon him and his fellow villagers, and damn anybody who might rock the boat and ruin it for everybody else. In Ryan's Bar Dunphy ruled and that's all there was to it. Dunphy turned on one of the gas lamps above the bar and started to clean another glass.

"You'd better drink a few more pints tonight, Vincent my boy," teased Dunphy, "because from tomorrow I'm putting up the price by another penny. So get it while it's cheap, that's all I can say."

Vincent recovered the power of speech as he slid from the stool and retrieved his money.

"Seven pennies a pint? You're out of your mind. You don't think people will pay that kind of money, do you? I certainly won't, that's for sure." Vincent stomped towards the door.

"Then take your business elsewhere, Vincent Corrigan. There are plenty of people who are more than glad to pay the going price for a decent pint of beer around here. More than enough, of that you can be sure."

Vincent returned and leaned forward over the bar.

"And who might those poor misguided wretches be?"

Dunphy nodded towards Joe and the other two as Vincent slammed the bar in anger.

"So that's your game, is it? Put up the prices while the Yanks swan around as if they own the place, then when they've gone put the price back down again. In the meantime you've fleeced half the village and all your friends at the same time."

Dunphy meticulously erased a non-existent smudge from the bottom of another glass with the damp tea towel.

"Now then, Vincent me boy," he said with practised insolence, "who said anything about putting it back to the same price?" Vincent looked to the musicians in the hope they might rally to the cause but there were no volunteers. He walked to the door then turned to address Dunphy one last time.

"You know what you are, Dunphy? You're a capitalist, that's what you are, nothing but a filthy capitalist. And you Quinn," he shouted, pointing to the musicians on the other side of the pub, "all of you, you should be ashamed of yourselves for encouraging him. And as for you lot," Vincent waved his fist at Joe, Gene and Bo, "you can go to the devil for all I care. You've caused nothing but trouble since you came here and the sooner you go back to Yankland the better."

Vincent threw open the door and left the pub with one final proclamation.

"I'll not stay in this den of thieves a moment longer."

"Good riddance then," said Dunphy as the door slammed shut behind Vincent.

Quinn and his musicians chuckled to themselves as Dunphy wiped the *7d* from the board and changed it back to *6d*. Gene and Bo emptied their glasses but Joe's thirst had lost its edge after the confrontation with Vincent.

Gene tried to catch his attention as Joe stared off into the distance.

"You ready for another?" Joe shook his head.

"What's wrong? You were full of beans a couple of minutes ago. Don't tell me she's getting to you already. Wait 'til you've dated her a few times then you can start looking like you're married."

Joe shrugged.

"It's nothing to do with Heather, it's just this is the first time I'm starting to get the feeling some people would maybe prefer we weren't here."

"Don't listen to what that old goat had to say," said Bo. "You ask most of the people in the village, they're real glad to have us around. Ain't that the truth, Michael?" Bo asked of Dunphy, getting up from the table with the empty glasses and walking across to the bar for a refill. Dunphy nodded in vigorous agreement as he poured the drinks. Bo indicated the chalkboard behind the bar.

"See that board? When they get some of that electricity in here Michael's gonna wire up a neon sign with a counter on it and change his prices at the press of a button. None of this scraping and scratching on a blackboard like some goddam caveman. And that calls for a toast." Bo picked up his glass and held it aloft.

"To progress," he said. Quinn and the others mumbled from the back of the bar in kind. Bo handed Gene his drink as Joe stood up.

"I'm heading back to..."

Gene and Bo both pulled Joe down onto his chair.

"Oh no you don't." said Gene. "You've been running around for the last couple of weeks like a lovesick moron ever since you set eyes on that girl and now you've finally got up the nerve to talk to her we're gonna celebrate."

Gene emptied his glass with one swallow and wiped his mouth with the back of his hand. Bo followed suit then handed his empty glass to Joe. "And you're buying. Again." ordered Bo. As a reluctant Joe slowly walked over to the bar the door swung open to reveal John Wayne and his drinking companion-in-crime, Victor McLaglen.

Wayne gently pushed Joe aside and slapped a five punt note onto the bar.

"This one's on me, Joe. Give me a couple of them black beers, barkeep, and serve these fine gentlemen friends of mine too, if you will. Tell me when we've drunk this," Wayne said, pushing the money towards Dunphy.

McLaglen reached over the bar and slid the note back towards Wayne.

"Your money's no good in here, Yank. I'll be getting these."

Wayne frowned for a moment then clicked his fingers.

"Don't you say something like that to me just before I punch you through the door of Cohan's Bar?" McLaglen nodded.

"I'm living the part, Duke, it helps me remember the lines."

"Yeah, well don't get too carried away, McLaglen. Let's confine the fist-fighting to when we're in front of the cameras, understand?"

"I'll do my best, Duke, but these black beers pack a bit of a wallop on their own, if you get what I'm saying."

Wayne wagged a thick finger in McLaglen's face.

"Two things. First of all, Mr Victor Andrew de Bier Everleigh McLaglen, you can drop that 'Oirish' accent of yours. We both know you're English. And secondly, no fighting. Not tonight, you hear me? In case you've forgotten you retired from boxing over forty years ago."

"Don't you worry, Marion," said McLaglen, impishly referring to Wayne by his real name. "I'll be on my best behaviour tonight". Wayne fixed his co-star with a murderous glare as McLaglen stared straight ahead, sipping at his drink and ostentatiously smacking his lips.

Eventually they sauntered over to join Gene and the others. Joe buried his face in his hands. It was going to be a long night.

Thomas knelt in silent prayer as the evening faded and darkness stole through the bedroom curtains. A small candle by the side of the bed painted his giant flickering shadow onto the wall. He wore one of his absent father's night shirts, which was at least three sizes too big but thick enough to keep out the chill of the evening. When the cold sometimes brushed his face and woke him in the night, Thomas would huddle down beneath the blankets, gather the collar of the night shirt close to his face and smell the garment, hoping it might reveal some lingering trace or residue of his father.

Every so often he thought he could smell the faint whiff of cigarette smoke, or the cologne his father wore on special occasions. Then Thomas would remember him, his features sharp and clear as if he had only just laid eyes upon his da moments before, instead of over two years ago. His eyes would sting with tears for a second or two as Thomas held on to the hope that one day Patrick would reappear and everything could be as before.

Offering up one last prayer for his father's return, Thomas ran to the bedroom door and opened it slightly to make sure he could hear if his mother came up the stairs. He returned to his bed and pulled a tattered Roy Rogers comic from beneath the mattress, then threw a quick glance heavenwards, just in case he was being monitored from above as well. A picture of Roy astride his famous horse Trigger adorned the cover. Jumping into bed Thomas opened the comic and began to read quietly to himself.

"Say pardner, the sheriff's taken a posse over to Devil's Canyon to track down Jake Skelton and his gang. That means we can rustle some of old man Cleaton's cattle tonight."

As Thomas turned the page he adopted a deep villainous voice and frowned, pushing his face down into his chest.

"Sure. With the sheriff out of town there won't be anybody to stop us."

He smiled to himself.

"Oh yes there will," he thought. "Oh yes there will."

He froze as his mother's voice suddenly rang out from the bottom of the stairs.

"Time to go to sleep now, Thomas. Out with that candle now."

He dropped the comic onto the bed.

"But mother, I'm reading."

"You can do that at school. Night time is for sleeping. Blow out that candle before it burns down any more. I'm not made of money, you know."

Thomas leaned over and extinguished the flame. A faint glimmer of light made its way through the gap in the curtains from a small gas lamp outside in the street. Thomas pulled the bedclothes over his head and from under his pillow retrieved a small battery-operated torch borrowed from Billy McNee. He switched on the torch and resumed the adventures of Roy Rogers, which culminated in the usual climactic shootout, after which Roy bathed his wounded head in the creek, Skelton's bullet having only creased his scalp.

Thomas closed the comic and switched off the torch in disgust.

"Shot again. He's got more holes in him than all my socks put together. Give me John Wayne any day."

Wayne sank his fourth pint of the evening then called to Quinn and the other musicians.

"You guys play those things or are you just gonna sit there all night tuning up? How about a couple of real old Irish songs, something to bring a tear to your mother's eye? Whaddya say?"

Quinn and his fellow players made their way across the near empty pub and sat by Wayne and the others.

"How about Galway Bay?" Wayne requested. McLaglen threw Quinn a sly wink.

"They've never heard of that one, have you boys?" Quinn shook his head.

"You don't know Galway Bay?" asked a surprised Wayne.

The four musicians shrugged in feigned ignorance. Wayne and Bo started to sing.

> *If you ever go across the sea to Ireland*
> *Then maybe at the closing of the day*

*You will sit and watch the moon rise over Cladach
And see the sun go down on Galway Bay.*

Gene and Joe provided the refrain.

On Galway Bay.

They looked to Quinn expectantly. He pushed out his bottom lip and shook his head once more.
"Okay, okay," Gene said. "How about I'll Take You Home, Kathleen? You must know that one."
McLaglen took a long drink and fixed his eyes on Quinn.
"I'll not have heard that one before," said Quinn with a poker face. As McLaglen put his glass down Joe caught the actor giving Quinn a quick thumbs-up sign. It took Joe just two seconds to decide it wasn't worth spoiling McLaglen's little game. Victor was a big man. Gene gave a sweet rendition of the sentimental Irish ballad.

*I'll take you home again, Kathleen
Across the ocean wild and wide
To where your heart has never been
Since 'ere you were my bonny bride.*

Gene looked to Quinn.

"No?" Quinn looked nonplussed. Bo decided to give it a try.

"How about Danny Boy? Don't tell you've never heard of that one."

The musicians' silence said it all. Wayne frowned.

"The Wild Rover?" asked Gene. Again no answer. Joe threw in a title.

"Dublin Town?" No answer. Gene shook his head in disbelief.

"Alright, alright, you must know this one," said Gene impatiently, starting to sing.

> *There was a wild colonial boy*
> *Jack Duggan was his name.*

Wayne, Bo and Joe joined in.

> *He was born and raised in Ireland*
> *In a place called Castlemaine.*

A deafening silence descended upon the bar as the four of them stopped singing. Quinn picked up his glass and drained it. The fiddler, the accordionist and the washboard player followed suit, placing their empty glasses before them. Wayne laughed then turned to Dunphy who stood watching the proceedings with glee as he leaned up against the bar, his chin resting on the palms of his hands.

"Okay, barkeep. Black beers for everybody." McLaglen and

Quinn exchanged a smile. The players' power of recall miraculously returned as they started to sing and play along with Wayne and the others.

> *He was his father's only son*
> *And his mothers pride and joy*
> *And dearly did his parent's love*
> *The wild colonial boy.*

They sang long and hard into the night, Wayne, the 'Quiet Man', the loudest of them all.

CHAPTER TWO

The following day found Dermot Gallagher doing what he did almost every morning since his father had seen fit to thoughtlessly pass away almost fifteen years before - wash his face in a bowl of cold water in the kitchen sink while his seventy-three-year-old mother, Minnie, sat in the corner reminding him of his failure to marry and procreate.

"You're the only one left to carry on the name of Gallagher," whined Minnie, drinking milk noisily from a tin cup. "It's your duty to pass on your seed..."

Gallagher tried to shut out his mother's presence by squeezing his eyes shut and cleaning his ears as thoroughly as possible in an effort to dull his hearing. Nothing however could erase from his mind the images his mother conjured up day after day when questioning his inability to procreate and produce an heir. Huddled in her chair by the window with her knitting needles and toothless grin, it had occurred to him many years before that his mother would not have looked out of place ensconced within the shadow of the guillotine in revolutionary France.

"Mother," her son remonstrated, quickly buttoning up his shirt in an effort to get out of the house and distance himself from Minnie as soon as possible, "my seed is my own business. Now please, not today, okay? Just let the matter rest for once. That's not too much to ask, is it?"

"You're no good to anybody when you're six feet in the ground," she said. "That's what your father used to say." Gallagher turned away from his mother, muttering to himself.

"That's because my father was no good to anybody when he was alive, apart from the bookmaker."

"Your father was a very wise man," insisted Minnie.

Except when it came to backing the horses, thought Dermot.

Minnie went on.

"He said to me once, he said, *Minnie,* he said, *life's too short not to make the most of it,* that's what he said. And do you know what he said to me after that?"

Dermot didn't have to ask. He'd heard Minnie say it a million times over since the funeral. With his back turned to his mother Dermot mouthed his dead father's words of wisdom as Minnie repeated them for the umpteenth time.

"He said to me, *Minnie,* he said, *I've met a lot of people in my time but I've never met anybody who's ever been here more than once.* That's what he said. And never was a truer word spoken."

Dermot nodded and threw back his cold cup of tea and made a dash for the door, calling out to his mother on the way.

"Got to go, mother. I'm off to attend a very important meeting. Bye." Minnie threw him some more advice just as he closed the door: "Try that lady who's in the film they're making, Maureen O'Hara. She'd make someone a lovely wife."

Dermot was halfway up the street before he realised that was the first thing he'd heard his mother say in the last twenty years that he actually agreed with.

A meeting had been called that day to discuss how the village might celebrate the arrival of electricity to the community and it fell to Dermot Gallagher, the master of ceremonies, to oversee the arrangements for the occasion in question. A self-appointed master of ceremonies if the truth be told, but for all that Gallagher was the right man for the job. At least that's the way Gallagher saw it. He felt he had forged a name for himself in the small community of Cong as a man who got things done – although his mother might not necessarily agree. The fact that he might occasionally profit from the process of 'getting things done' was neither here nor there as far as he was concerned, and Gallagher most certainly intended to profit from the introduction of electricity as much as possible.

It was therefore to his advantage to ensure the relationship between the electricity board and the villagers went smoothly and without fuss. Particularly as Jack Boone, the local site inspector for the ESB, would also be present at the meeting.

To that end Gallagher had put on his best Sunday suit, determined to show the people of Cong that he was more than capable of representing their interests with the bureaucratic Boone. The fact that he and Boone already enjoyed a clandestine business relationship, with regard to the supply of electrical goods, was something he was at pains to keep to himself.

The fact that he also had no real competition in the ironmongery business for a radius of approximately fifty miles or more was irrelevant. It was winning the game that counted, he would often to say to himself, even when there was no other team to play against.

Gallagher nodded and murmured his way up the aisle of the hall. The villagers sat on opposite sides of an invisible line of demarcation that neither faction wished to acknowledge. Catholic and Protestant alike revelled in their ability to live side by side in a state of harmony and neighbourly love rarely seen outside the confines of Cong. The priests, however, viewed things quite differently, insisting that the Church of Ireland sat to the left of the hall, with the Holy Catholic Church of Rome on the right. It was quite fitting therefore that Gallagher should find himself walking down the middle.

He was religious by default, but not by personal choice. The infighting and constant sniping between both sides contributed to his conviction that religion was a curse to those who worshipped, and a convenient tool for those who practised it for a living in order to subjugate the gullible masses.

Gallagher stepped onto the raised platform at the end of the hall. At one end of the stage sat Father William Donnelly, shepherd of the Catholic flock. At the other end sat Reverend Roderick Casey, belligerent warden of the Church of Ireland. Reverend Casey's seventy-year-old face was almost obscured by a large set of bushy eyebrows underlined by a thin-lipped gash of a mouth that roared and poured forth hell and damnation every Sunday morning upon those sinners who dared to enter the house of the Lord. By his book that covered about practically everybody in the congregation. He exercised an expression of devilish severity upon those who sat directly in front of him in order to ensure no one spoke out of turn without his express permission.

Father Donnelly on the other hand could not have looked more relaxed as he leaned back in his chair, feet crossed beneath the table and twiddling his thumbs. In his late twenties, Donnelly was fairly new to the community and had yet to inveigle his way into the hearts and souls of those who worshipped the Lord above all else, including the Catholics. His beaming red face and boyish charm had endeared him to a lot of the women in the village, including some, it was said in whispered tones, who worshipped at the Church of Ireland. Gallagher sat between the priests with Jack Boone to his left. Boone, a thin sour-faced looking individual in his mid-forties and an ill-fitting suit, surveyed the gathering with a thin smile.

Gallagher rapped the table with his knuckles to silence the mutterings within the hall. As he raised himself to his fullest inconsiderable height, the young Father Donnelly rose and pipped him to the post.

"Ladies and gentlemen, although there are a number of you here today that I do not recognise from my usual flock," he said, smiling, "I feel confident we are all united in a common cause, determined that as a community we can all learn to live together and share in the..."

Gallagher tugged at Father Donnelly's sleeve and pulled him back into his chair.

"Father, this is a village hall, not a church. Now please, we have a number of things that need to be..."

Reverend Casey stood to have his say. "Electricity is the work of the devil, mark my words. No good will come of it, you can be sure of that."

This sentiment was greeted by a few random claps of general agreement from his obedient flock.

"And if the man from the ESB and his partners in crime aren't Catholic spawn," he continued, pointing at a rather bemused Boone, "then I'll eat my hat."

Both parties in the segregated congregation renewed age-old hostilities and started pointing and gesticulating angrily across the aisle in between. Gallagher tried to quieten the crowd but the meeting appeared to be falling apart before it had even begun. Order slowly resumed as Father Donnelly rose to address the crowd once more with what could be taken for a genial nod towards his opposite number.

"Now that the ESB have finally seen fit to bring to us the miracle of electricity we must look to the future, not the past. It is important that we share in the prosperity and the many opportunities available to this wonderful little community of ours, and it must be shared willingly. Without hesitation or rancour."

Father Donnelly moved to sit in his chair as his sentiments found favour with all those in the hall including a somewhat suspicious Reverend Casey.

"Except of course with the heathen swine sitting on the other side of the hall over there," added Father Donnelly.

Pandemonium erupted between the now openly warring factions as Gallagher rapped on the table, ignored by all. His stomach lurched as he realised he might very well lose complete control of the meeting. Father Donnelly and Reverend Casey stood shouting at each other from either side of the platform while Gallagher and Boone shook their heads in unified resignation. The audience stood in reverent silence as the two opposing men of God played out their prejudices in front of everyone.

"It will bring warmth to every house..." asserted Father Donnelly.

"Crop failure, more like it," countered a red-faced Reverend Casey.

"Hot water at the turn of a tap..."

"Death to every single cow, sheep, pig and any other living creature of God within a twenty-mile radius."

"Alternative methods of heating..."

"Every peat cutter out on his arse," a now puce-coloured Reverend Casey shouted back. Despite his lack of belief in all things great and wise Gallagher felt things were going too far when priests swore and cursed with alacrity.

"Fathers, if you please!" he cried. The priests sat down like marionettes suddenly detached from their strings. The thunderous scraping of chairs on the once finely polished village hall floor filled the air as the congregation also slowly sat down.

Gallagher reached for the silk handkerchief that flopped from his breast pocket and wiped his brow. He pointed towards both priests at the same time, dividing a stern look between the two of them.

"One more word and I shall have to ask both of you to leave the hall. Carrying on like this, what kind of example are you setting to the people here? It's enough to turn the saints agnostic."

The priests sat in suitably chastised silence. Gallagher cleared his throat and began to speak in what he considered to be the assured tones of a practised after-dinner speaker, with an opening address that he had rehearsed many times in front of his bedroom mirror.

"I would like to talk about the arrangements for the coming festivities to celebrate the arrival of electricity to the village. But before I do so the local representative for the ESB, Mr Boone here, wishes to say a few words. Mr Boone."

Boone stood with his hands gripping his lapels in a manner more befitting a head teacher addressing a class of unruly school children.

"Father, Reverend, Mr Gallagher, ladies and gentlemen, first of all I'd like to say how delighted we are at the ESB that the community in Cong have welcomed us here with open arms – indeed, open hearts as well. The ESB therefore thought it only right that I be present here today to answer any final questions you might have in relation to the..."

Boone stopped as Gerald O'Brien raised his hand from the back of the hall. A scruffy and ill-mannered man in his late thirties, O'Brien lolled against the wall in his black donkey jacket and blue canvas trousers, a large pair of black Wellington boots completing a picture of irrefutable sartorial elegance. At least to those in pig-farming circles.

"You thought it what, Mr Boone, sir?" asked O'Brien.

The congregation turned as one towards the back of the hall. For a few seconds they displayed unity, groaning in dismay at O'Brien's presence as he planted one of his muddy boots upon the wall behind him. Boone looked to the ceiling and quietly counted to three before responding.

"Prudent. Judicious. Sensible. Sagacious even," replied Boone as he supplied a number of synonyms associated with the word in question. "Is that clear, Mr O'Brien?" he asked.

O'Brien pulled at an invisible peaked cap in sarcastic deference.

"Clear enough, squire, clear enough," replied O'Brien. Boone smiled through clenched teeth as he continued.

"I thought it prudent to answer any questions you might have about the introduction of electricity and the opportunities it will bring..."

O'Brien pushed himself away from the wall angrily as he interrupted Boone once more.

"Such as the opportunity to buy electrical goods from Gallagher's store at exorbitant prices. Is that what you mean, Mr Boone, sir?"

Gallagher rose to defend himself. "How do you know...?"

"This is a small village, Gallagher. Don't think nobody knows what you're really up to."

"You're just put out because the ESB didn't want to compensate you for running the wires across that field of yours, that's what's getting to you, isn't it, Mr O'Brien?" spluttered Gallagher. "You had a chance to have your say two years ago when the ESB said they'd be routing the power into Connemara in the first place. Now either shut up or get out!"

O'Brien turned on his feet and, with a loud squelch of combined mud and farmyard droppings, left the hall to the sound of barely suppressed applause. Boone and Gallagher exchanged looks of immense relief at his swift exit.

Relief because his line of questioning threatened to be not only detrimental to Gallagher's standing in the community but also jeopardised Boone's ambition to retire at an early age with his cut of the proceeds from the goods sold by his newly acquired business partner, one Dermot Gallagher. Just as Gallagher was about to continue his address O'Brien walked right back into the hall again.

"And another thing, I'd like to know what you and everybody else are going to do about these gentlemen from Hollywood walking around this village of ours as if they own the place."

Gallagher stepped into the fray once more.

"They have brought more money into this town in the space of the last few weeks than anyone's brought here in the last two years," he bellowed.

"I don't see any of it going into my pocket."

Gallagher adopted the posture akin to that of an aggressive schoolboy as he leaned forward with his hands tucked into his sides.

"Well that's because nobody wanted a miserable old sod like you in their film now, did they? Turned you down flat when they were casting for extras last week, isn't that right, Mr James Cagney?"

O'Brien pointed to Gallagher with cynical smile.

"Nice suit you're wearing there, Mr Gallagher, sir. Made in Hollywood?"

O'Brien left the hall without waiting for a response. Gallagher made sure he wasn't able to return by striding to the back of the hall and slamming the door shut. He turned and addressed the gathering from his position by the door.

"Are there any questions for Mr Boone?" A number of hands rose from the middle of the crowd then retreated as Gallagher hurried the proceedings along.

"No? Right. Thank you for your time, Mr Boone." Boone stood and rushed from the platform.

"The pleasure was all mine, Mr Gallagher. Good day to you all," he called out, waving his bowler hat as he made his way towards the exit. Gallagher opened the door for him as they shook hands, almost pushing Boone out of the hall before anybody summoned up the wherewithal to try throwing another question about the ESB at either of them.

Gallagher thought it wise to keep his business partnership with Boone under wraps. The villagers looked with suspicion upon anybody from the outside who might profit from their community in any way whatsoever. Unless, of course, everybody got a fair share. Gallagher hurried back to the raised platform to conclude the main business of the day.

"Right. On to more important matters. The festivities. In a week's time the ESB will have laid down the lines in order to bring more than enough power to light up all the houses and streets in Cong. With plenty left over to illuminate every single room in Ashford Castle as well. And I think that's something well worth celebrating."

General murmurs of agreement rippled through the audience. Gallagher continued.

"I have taken it upon myself to invite Mr John Ford, Mr John Wayne, Mr Ward Bond, the lovely Miss Maureen O'Hara..." Gallagher started to straighten his tie and smooth his hair, silently communicating his feelings for the fiery actress. "...and, of course, Mr Victor McLaglen to join us in a suitable venue to help commemorate this auspicious occasion."

Michael Dunphy, a fully paid up Catholic, raised his hand from the front row.

"I'd like to take the opportunity to humbly volunteer Ryan's Bar as the chosen venue for just such an occasion, if I may."

Gallagher frowned at the barman. The thought of inviting Maureen O'Hara to a pub was going beyond the realms of common decency.

"Mr Dunphy, I am not talking about a common bar. These celebrations should take place in a more suitable..."

"And as a matter of course," interjected Dunphy, "we'll be donating at least four barrels of beer to..."

"Six," said Gallagher.

"Done," said Dunphy.

"That's agreed then," said Gallagher as he brought the meeting to a close. "Ryan's Bar it is."

Reverend Casey jumped up from his seat with an agility that belied his age and stepped down from the platform to lead his side of the hall out of the building first. Father Donnelly watched in bemusement as the members of the Church of Ireland shuffled down the aisle in single file, his hands tucked behind his head as if he were sitting on a deckchair in the hot midday sun. As Reverend Casey reached the door Gallagher called out from the stage.

"And make sure you all wear your Sunday best on the day. We may be poor but we don't have to dress like it."

Outside the meeting, O'Brien accosted Jack Boone just as the man from the ESB was climbing into his car.

"We had a deal," O'Brien reminded him, leaning on the side of the vehicle with his dirty boot perched on the running board.

Boone wound down the driver's window.

"We had nothing of the sort, O'Brien, and you know it. I said I would do whatever I could to facilitate payment for routing the wires across your land if it were in the interests of the ESB. I made no promises."

O'Brien leaned down and glared through the window at Boone.

"You said the ESB..."

"They had a budget and a schedule to keep," Boone said. "It would have been prohibitive to have to pay every Tom, Dick or Harry every time they wanted to plant poles in some farmer's backyard."

"Fifty fifty. On completion of the deal. Remember?"

Boone started the car, then spoke as if addressing a small child.

"They had a schedule. I tried my best but they were having none of it. Now move away from the car. Good day to you."

O'Brien slowly removed his foot from the running board.

"Well, Mr Boone, we can't go upsetting their schedule now, can we? By the way, rumour has it that you and Gallagher are partners."

Boone nearly stalled the car in shock. O'Brien wasn't slow in realising he had touched a nerve.

"You're still leaning on my vehicle," Boone pointed out. "and I would advise you to let the matter drop. I am assured that the electricity will arrive in the village on time - as scheduled -

and that's an end to the matter."

As Boone drove off O'Brien swung his leg at the boot of the vehicle in cold fury.

"I think you might be a little bit wrong there, Mr Boone, if I may say so myself. The matter isn't over yet. Not until I say so, or my name isn't Gerald Michael Collins O'Brien."

Further up the street, at the bottom of the main road that led through the village, stood a stone High Cross of indeterminate age. It was to this cross in the hot Saturday midday sun that Joe, Gene and Bo silently prayed for relief from the alcoholic damage they had inflicted upon themselves the night before.

All three struggled in their efforts to help set up a shot in which John Wayne and Maureen O'Hara ride a tandem down the hill of the main street. Out of the corner of his eyes Joe saw Thomas, Billy and Michael sitting on the wall opposite, watching as the crew prepared the lights and camera equipment.

Joe climbed into the cab of the generator van, which was parked across the middle of the street, nursing the worst hangover he had ever had. Since the last one, anyway. He only hoped that Gene and Bo were equally as fragile as he witnessed the both of them connecting up the powerful Klieg lights that towered high above the road.

At Gene's signal Joe turned over the engine to power up the

generator. The huge lamps flared up, the powerful beams bathing the already sunlit road in a shimmering glow that hovered just above the cracked surface of the highway.

While the crew busied themselves getting everything ready for the imminent arrival of Ford and the actors, a lorry laden with piles of cut peat drove down the hill towards them. Sean McKee pulled to a stop in front of the generator van. He was a small unshaven man in his early fifties, his teeth yellowed by too many cigarettes, one of which dangled half smoked from his lips as he took in the scene of apparent chaos that blocked his way. McKee leaned out of the cab and called to Gene.

"Would you mind clearing the way there now? There's no room for me to get past." Gene wiped his aching brow and nodded to Bo.

"You do this," he pleaded through a parched mouth. "I only have sight in one eye at the moment. And be nice."

A perspiring Bo stumbled over to the lorry.

"Excuse me?" enquired Bo.

McKee pointed to all the equipment in the middle of the road.

"I was saying, I need to get round all of - all of this - whatever this is. I have to use the road for the vehicle."

Bo scratched his head and sighed.

"Look, we've been setting up here for the last two hours. Can't you go round another way, huh?" pleaded Bo.

McKee jumped out of the vehicle. His shirt sleeves were

practically rolled up to his shoulders, the veins on his thick brown stocky arms accentuated by the glow of the lights. He took one last drag then flicked the cigarette over Bo's shoulder.

The crew stopped working as both men squared off to each other while Thomas and his friends sat witnessing the confrontation a few feet away. Bo was not much taller than McKee, but he looked a great deal wider than the nimble little man who stood before him. McKee pushed his cap back and moved closer to Bo.

"I'm not prepared to go three miles out of my way just so you can avoid being inconvenienced, you follow me? I have the right of way on this road and I'll drive down any street I want. And right now I want to drive down this one. Do you understand me now?"

Bo kept his eyes fixed on McKee, who gave the impression he was about to pounce at any moment, and called out to Joe.

"Joe. When's the old man coming down?"

"He's due about now, I reckon," answered Joe, suddenly turning in panic should Ford suddenly creep up on him unawares.

Bo cursed under his breath. The tension was almost visible in the air as the huge lights continued to beat down upon the hapless Bo and the irate lorry driver.

"Look, mister," Bo pleaded, "I'd like to help you, really I

would. If it were down to me I'd move this stuff for you with my own bare hands. But our director's going to be awful upset if things aren't just the way he wants them to be so what do you say you cut me some slack. How's about it, huh fella?"

McKee moved slightly closer, his eyes a blank. The onlookers held their breath as Bo stood his ground.

"You know, I would really appreciate it if you could see your way clear to kind of backing up that lorry of yours and..."

McKee poked Bo in the chest. Gene closed his eyes and waited for the sound of fist on face.

"I don't care about your big Hollywood director, all I want…"

To everybody's relief, including Joe, John Ford's large black Customline Ford came around the corner and parked next to the generator van. Ford clambered from the passenger seat wearing a casual tweed jacket, and a pair of light trousers, a silk handkerchief tucked in the top pocket of the jacket and the 'other' handkerchief dangling from the pocket of his trousers. He also sported a flat white cap, a pipe, the usual pair of dark glasses and the ever-present scowl.

"Morning, Mr Ford," Joe said in a loud attempt to sound sparkling and fresh. Ford scowled again.

"What's the problem here?" demanded Ford. Once again Joe's friends deserted him in his hour of need. He pinched his brow in the hope that the man drilling through his forehead from the inside might desist for just a moment or two while he attempted to explain the situation.

"Well you see, sir, this man," he pointed to McKee. "wants to drive that lorry there," he indicated the vehicle laden with peat. "through all the stuff we've spent most of the morning setting up right here. Which means that the man with the lorry over there..."

Ford suddenly walked over to the driver as Joe waved his arms back and forth. He held out his hand to greet McKee.

"I'm the guy in charge around here. Are these people causing you any problems?"

Joe could see McKee visibly relax the minute Ford addressed him. Mainly because Ford had suddenly adopted an Irish accent.

"I wouldn't say it was inconveniencing me too much now but I'd be much obliged if you could get your boys to let me through."

Ford turned to Joe.

"Move it," he instructed.

Joe started the engine as Bo, Gene and the rest of the crew obeyed Ford without

question, moving the cables back from the middle of the road along with the lights.

Ford walked his new friend back to the peat lorry.

"Say, where you from?" he asked, placing his arm gently on McKee's shoulder.

"I originally hail from Carraroe but these days I live over in Moycullen," McKee told him.

"Carraroe in Galway Bay?"

"The very same," said McKee as he climbed up into the driver's seat.

Ford nodded.

"I was born in Spiddal," the director said, his Irish accent becoming even more and more pronounced.

"You don't say now? What's a feller like you doing all the way up here then?"

"Trying to scratch a living just like everybody else," said Ford.

The crew hurriedly wheeled all of the equipment clear of the road.

"You drive careful now," said Ford, tapping the door of the lorry with his pipe.

"Thank you for your kindness, sir. Very much appreciated."

McKee started the vehicle and slowly drove down the hill. Ford suddenly stepped up onto the running board and spoke to McKee in a shout, his voice loud enough to be heard above the noise of the engine and pointed to the shop on the corner of the hill with Cohan's Bar painted above it.

"By the way, see that bar there?"

McKee shook his head.

"That's not a bar. It's a shop."

"Used to be a shop. We've turned it into a real bar. Next time

65

you're driving through, stop off in there and get yourself a drink on me. Tell 'em to put it on John Ford's slate. They'll know who I am."

McKee held his thumb aloft in a gesture of appreciation.

"You're a gentleman, sir, a real gentleman."

McKee gunned the engine and drove out of the village. Ford glared at the crew.

"What are you all looking at? I said I wanted this set ready by noon. You've got thirty minutes, then we shoot."

Thomas and his friends had sat watching the little drama unfolding before them with

keen interest. Thomas in particular was quite spellbound by the power that Ford appeared to wield over the crew. With startling clarity he suddenly knew what he wanted to be when he grew up. He wanted to be John Ford. Apart from the bullying and the shouting and the habitual moaning it looked like a pretty good job to Thomas from where he was standing. He turned to Billy and Michael.

"Did you hear that? He lied to that man about Cohan's Bar."

"Maybe it was a joke," Billy suggested.

"Or maybe," said Michael, "he might not know himself it's not a bar."

"He must do" said Thomas. "He's the director."

"Directors don't know everything," asserted Michael.

"Maybe it was a joke," said Billy again.

Thomas and Michael thought about this for a moment, both reaching the same conclusion at the same time.

"Nah," they chorused. Their attention was then distracted by the arrival of another chauffeured car which parked next to Ford's vehicle. A woman with flaming red hair and a very tall well built man climbed out of the vehicle. Thomas was unable to contain his excitement at the sight of John Wayne in the flesh.

"Look! Look! It's the man himself. It's John Wayne!" he cried.

'Wayne' turned and waved to the boys, smiling and shaking his head at the same time. Michael poked Thomas in the ribs.

"That's not him, you fool. It's his stunt man. His stand-in they call him. The real John Wayne's probably back at the castle, sleeping it off."

"What do you mean, his stunt man?" asked an appalled Thomas. He had got his father to take him to see every John Wayne movie possible whenever the films were shown over Claremorris or Ballinrobe, or even by the travelling cinemas that on occasion passed through the village, and was resolute in his conviction. "John Wayne does his own stunts," he said. "I read it."

"Does all his own drinking is more like it," said Michael in a knowing tone. "My old man reckons he can really put it away when he wants. Says he's a real regular feller, though."

Thomas was still horrified that Wayne would have recourse to a stunt man.

"I don't believe it! Why should he need a stunt man? What are those people going to be doing that's so dangerous? Tell me that, clever clogs."

Michael shrugged.

"Don't ask me. Maybe he's going to have to kiss the girl."

He and Billy dissolved into fits of laughter, Billy puckering his lips and kissing the air.

"They kiss? Uuugh," said Thomas in disgust.

Billy's face took on a look of deep concern.

"I didn't know John Wayne was married to the woman in the film," he said. Michael scoffed.

"They're not, stupid!"

Thomas begged to differ.

"They must be. If they're kissing they have to be married."

"Why?" demanded Michael.

"Because me mother says so," replied Thomas, Billy nodding in agreement. "She says if two people kiss they have to be married first. It's a sin otherwise."

"Don't be daft," sneered Michael. "They're actors. They don't kiss for real."

"How do you not kiss for real?" asked a perplexed Billy.

"Easy," said Michael with an air of superiority. "Like this."

Michael's cheeks disappeared as he sucked his lips into his

mouth. For added effect he crossed his eyes as well and made a kissing sound. Billy laughed again. Thomas wasn't convinced.

"It's not for real if you don't use your lips. Honest."

Thomas finished the argument once and for all by quoting his mother. She would have the last word as usual even if she wasn't there.

"My ma says it's a sin. And I never argue with my ma, especially when she's wrong. Now you see that feller over there?" he said, pointing to a half-dead Joe. "He's sweet on my sister. Let's ask him if the real John Wayne is going to be here today."

Thomas jumped down from the wall and made his way across the road towards Joe. The two stand-ins sat astride a tandem next to the cross as the crew busied themselves with the lighting under Ford's instructions. As Thomas reached up to tap Joe on the elbow, he caught sight of a figure walking down the hill in the middle of the road.

Could it really be…?

The young boy narrowed his eyes against the sun and the bright lights that shone above him, as he tried to make out the identity of the shadowy speck of a man bearing down upon him. As the figure grew ever so slowly closer a jolt of recognition shot through Thomas and took his breath away as Patrick O'Dea walked up to his son and lifted him high into the air.

Thomas threw his arms around his father's neck and held on tight in case he should melt right before his eyes. Patrick walked over to the pavement and put Thomas down. He leaned over and patted his son on the head, Thomas still gulping for air while Patrick's eyes gleamed with a mixture of pride and regret.

"You've grown quite a bit, haven't you?" Patrick said. "The proper young man about town, ay?"

Thomas regained control of his breathing, his face flushed with emotion as he looked into his father's piercing blue eyes.

"Are you back now, da? Are you coming back for good? Are you staying?" he pleaded, still afraid his father might disappear at a moment's notice. Patrick stroked his son's hair as he watched the film crew setting up at the bottom of the hill.

"What's going on here, Tommy?" his father asked, staring around him incredulously at the sight of the camera and lighting equipment spread out across the village street.

Thomas's interest in the film, and anything to do with John Wayne, had evaporated with the magical return of his da.

"It's just a film, nothing special. Are you staying, da, are you staying?"

Patrick turned his attention back to Thomas.

"Tommy boy, I'm here to stay and that's a fact, so don't you be fretting. How's your mother and sister doing?".

"I think it's best you ask her that, da. Her and Heather, they've not been getting on too well these days."

"Where's your mother now?" Patrick asked, looking around.

"She took the bus down to Spiddal this morning to go see Auntie May. She won't be back 'til about tea time."

"And Heather?"

"She's gone with her. Gallagher gave her the day off special."

"She works at Gallagher's? I bet she's grown into a handsome looking young girl while I've been gone," said Patrick.

He stood up straight, his six-foot frame towering over his son. The cloth cap and ill-fitting black suit had seen better days, the arms of the jacket and the trouser legs a patchwork of mismatched material and amateur attempts to repair what remained of the original cloth. Anybody looking from a distance would see Patrick O'Dea for what he was, a man down on his luck and barely two coins to rub together. When Thomas looked he saw his father and he was glad of it. Patrick put his finger to his mouth.

"Look son, let's keep this our little secret for the moment, what do you say?" Thomas nodded.

"We'll give your mother and Heather a little surprise later on." Patrick rubbed his hands together as he looked across the street towards Ryan's Bar.

"In the meantime first things first. I need to see how that

rascal Michael Dunphy is doing. Do you fancy some lemonade on the old man?" Thomas nodded and smiled, unable to convey in words how happy he was to see his father again. He held onto Patrick's hand for dear life as they crossed the road together.

"I'll bring you out a drink in a minute. Now don't go away, you hear?" Thomas nodded obediently. Patrick reached into the battered canvas bag hanging from his back and produced a handful of comics. "Take a look at these, son. All the way from America". Thomas stared in wide-eyed wonder as he held about ten dog-eared cowboy comics in his hands, half featuring John Wayne, the others dedicated to Roy Rogers. He signalled to Billy and Michael to join him as Patrick entered the pub.

"Me da's back," said Thomas with pride. "And look! He's brung some John Wayne comics." Billy and Michael gathered excitedly around their friend, as Thomas placed the comics gently on the ground. "Give me a leg-up, both of you," implored Thomas. "I want to make sure he doesn't skip town again. There's a lemonade in it for you."

The two boys hoisted Thomas high enough for him to peer over the top of the half-frosted window pane into the pub.

Patrick crept into Ryan's bar. Two of Quinn's musician friends sat over in the far corner playing dominoes.

"The last time I saw you, Michael me boy, you were cleaning that very same glass.

Why don't you get yourself a sink like any other respectable watering hole?"

Patrick grinned as Dunphy caught his first sight of Thomas's father in nearly two years through the bottom of a murky beer glass. His jaw dropped open in amazement at the sheer effrontery of the man as Patrick clambered onto a stool and winked at him.

"This must be a first, Michael. Never known you to be tongue-tied. I've only been down the road for a little while and you've gone all bashful on me."

Dunphy shook his head in amused disbelief.

"That's because I've never known a man such as yourself with the barefaced cheek to come waltzing back into this village as if you've just popped down to the corner shop for an ounce of tobacco," Dunphy replied. "What did Mary have to say when she saw you?"

Patrick smiled ruefully.

"Thought I'd fortify the soul somewhat before I waltzed home, so to speak," he said, indicating the optics of whisky on the wall.

"Very wise, Patrick, very wise indeed. It'll also serve to dull the pain when she brains you with the steaming iron as well."

Patrick peered through the darkness towards the back of the

pub where a large banner with the words ESB WELCOMES CONG TO THE FOLD hung across the top of the wall.

"What's that all about then? Christmas come early?"

"They've finally got round to sending the electricity our way. Just think, Patrick, you won't have to go a'wandering no more in search of the bright lights. You'll have your very own right here in Cong," chided Dunphy.

"And that's reason enough to decorate the bar? You've never so much as hung a balloon up in this place before."

"When Cong goes electric next weekend the official celebrations are going to take place in this very establishment. I have personally arranged for the famous Hollywood cowboy star Mr John Wayne himself to extinguish the last gas lamp in Cong."

Patrick laughed.

"John Wayne? John Wayne, he says," nodding to the only other customers in the bar. "If you were going to go to all the trouble of getting somebody all the way over from Hollywood the least you could have done was get somebody Irish. Like Errol Flynn. John Wayne. Who are you kidding? He'd never come to a place like this. Look at it."

Dunphy shrugged

"The beautiful Miss Maureen O'Hara will then do us the honour of turning on the power to the village by throwing a switch which is to be placed over there, at the end of the bar.

At which point the festivities will begin. Festivities to which you are not invited, Patrick O'Dea, until such time as you humbly apologise for your cheap and derogatory remarks regarding this establishment and the famous clientele that choose to favour it."

The thought of mingling socially with Maureen O'Hara tempered Patrick's scorn somewhat.

"Maureen O'Hara? Now why didn't you say so in the first place?" he leered. "She can throw my switch any time she likes, if you get my meaning, Dunphy me boy. And I assume that the liquid refreshments will flow freely in every sense of the word?"

"Not in your direction it won't, you layabout."

"What's the chance of me maybe getting some work on this film then?" said Patrick, his eyes lighting up at the possibility of making some quick money.

"If I were pushed I'd have to say when hell freezes over," replied Dunphy, a malicious smile playing across his face. "They're here for a few more weeks but they've got all the help they need. I wouldn't even bother asking if I were you."

Patrick cursed.

"Just my luck."

Dunphy grinned so hard his cheeks nearly obscured his eyes.

"I'm sure Mary will be finding a few things for you to do around the house, ay Patrick?"

Patrick rapidly changed the subject.

"Er, Michael, be a friend and give me a lemonade for the boy and....". Patrick swivelled round on the stool "...shout the bar on me, will you Michael, there's a good feller."

Dunphy glared at Patrick while he opened a bottle of pop.

"Your ship come in yet, O'Dea?"

"On its way, Michael, on its way." Patrick took the lemonade and headed for the door. "In the meantime Michael, if you'd be so kind, on the slate if you please. Thanks."

Dunphy flushed with anger then took a deep breath as he pulled the pint he knew would never be paid for.

Patrick nearly tripped over the three boys sitting on the ground outside the pub, leaning against the wall and flicking quietly through the cowboy comics. "Ah, Tommy boy," exclaimed Patrick, handing the glass of lemonade to his grateful son, "you didn't say we had company. Two more lemonades coming up." Patrick turned to go back into the pub and froze momentarily as he came face-to-face with PC Flanagan. The officer stood imperiously in front of the village prodigal son, his hands clasped behind his back. Patrick quickly regained his composure and ceremoniously checked the scratched and worn watch on his left wrist.

"Not bad, Flanagan," said Patrick. "I've only been back five minutes and already you've come to wish me well."

"Bad news travels fast," replied the PC.

"Will you not be joining me for a drink, then?" queried Patrick with a false smile. "Celebrate my homecoming". It was now Flanagan's turn to battle with his own composure.

"The day I drink with your kind is the day I – it's the day I – well....," spluttered Flanagan.

"Never were too good at the old analogies there, were you, PC Flanagan?" taunted Patrick. "More concerned about wielding a big stick instead of concentrating on the lost art of eloquent speaking, I dare say." Patrick started to push open the pub door then turned once more to a red-faced Flanagan.

"By the way, Sherlock," asked Patrick, "did you ever solve the robbery of those ten barrels of beer from Hanratty's a couple of years back?"

"You mean the robbery that took place just before you disappeared off to sea again?" countered Flanagan. Patrick nodded his head and stroked his chin as if in deep thought.

"Now you come to mention it, I do believe the crime was committed just prior to the beginning of my last seafaring expedition. My. What a coincidence". Flanagan moved menacingly closer and pointed a bony finger in Patrick's face.

"Put just one foot wrong, O'Dea. For my sake. Please." Patrick called out as the PC turned away and walked back down the street.

"Hey, Flanagan. Seen my old lady recently?"

Flanagan kept on walking as Patrick taunted him. "She's too good for the likes of you, O'Dea," the PC replied over his shoulder. "Devil knows what she ever saw in you." Patrick threw a final barb just before entering the pub.
"Turned you down then, did she?" A stung Flanagan maintained his dignity and disappeared around the corner.

The three boys remained squat against the wall to the pub, mildly interested in the exchange between Patrick and Flanagan, but totally oblivious to the real meaning of the conversation they had just heard. Billy put down the Roy Rogers comic he was trying to read and pointed to the periodical in Thomas' hand. "When are you going to finish reading that John Wayne one?" he asked. Thomas remained engrossed in his comic as he answered Billy. "What's wrong with Roy Rogers? He's just as good a cowboy as John Wayne". "Not sure I like him that much," replied Billy. He nudged Michael in the ribs. "Who do you prefer? Roy Rogers or John Wayne?". Michael sighed and gave Billy a withering look of pity. "It's John Wayne hands-down as far as I'm concerned," averred Michael.
"Why's that?" asked both Thomas and Billy at the same time. Michael contemplated his thoughts for a moment as he scanned the Roy Rogers comic in his hands. Finally, he spoke. "Well, me da thinks he's too fond of his horse. Say's it's kind

of - unnatural." Thomas and Billy nodded sagely before returning to their comic books and, just like Michael, had no idea what he was going on about.

Vincent Corrigan had decided he would have nothing more to do with Ryan's Bar. Or Dunphy, for that matter. Not until that swindling thief of a barman took it upon himself to do the decent thing and charge a proper price for a pint of beer.

In the meantime, though, it meant he would probably burn in purgatory like the good lapsed Catholic he was, by satisfying his thirst in Hanratty's. Although the proprietor was a misguided Protestant, the beer was a damned sight more affordable.

The pub was located between the village hall and the corner of the hill where the High Cross stood. Vincent scowled at the film crew further up the road before making his way over the street and into Hanratty's.

As he was about to cross the street someone tapped Vincent on the shoulder from behind. Vincent whirled around with his fists curled to confront the juvenile spawn he expected to be making fun of him, only to find himself face to face with Quinn the musician. Quinn stepped back and held his hands up like a boxer, the two old men squaring up to each other like a couple of octogenarian pugilists.

"Steady on there, Vincent," said Quinn. "You were good in

your day but I'm at least two years younger and three to four hundred bottles of whisky lighter."

Vincent dropped his fists, sneering at Quinn before turning away.

"I used to eat flute players for breakfast. On your way." He turned to cross the road.

Quinn followed.

"Vincent. You missed a good one last night."

"What are you talking about, you tone deaf old ...?"

"That feller, John Wayne. Just after you left he came down to Ryan's. Bought everybody a drink. Twice."

Vincent cringed inside at the injustice of it all, his anger manifesting itself externally in the shape of a two-fingered salute to send the annoying little flute player on his way. "Ah, go across yourself," Vincent muttered. Quinn ignored the insult and pushed a little more.

"Twice, I tell you. Lovely feller."

While Vincent and Quinn indulged in their acrimonious tête-à-tête Wayne and Maureen O'Hara arrived on the set to take over from the stand-ins. The actors pushed the tandem up the hill past the three boys still stood outside Ryan's. Thomas was precariously balanced up against the window, Michael and Billy holding one foot each.

Michael turned to Billy.

"Was that John Wayne, do you think?"

Billy shrugged.

"I think that was John Wayne," asserted Michael. "Hey, Thomas, it's John Wayne, look."

Thomas waved his friend away as he pressed his nose up against the window.

"Sshh. I'm keeping an eye on me da. That's the second pint he's drunk in the last ten minutes."

"Suit yourself," said Michael.

Wayne and O'Hara sped past the boys down the hill towards the camera, O'Hara letting out a shrill cry of fearful excitement as the tandem picked up speed.

Vincent stepped into the street.

"I'm off to Hanratty's."

"What are you doing drinking in a place like that for?" asked Quinn. "It's full of Protestants and..."

"It's full of cheaper beer, that's all that concerns me. And don't go mixing drink with religion," threatened Vincent. "Otherwise I'll box your ears, you traitor."

As he reached the middle of the road Joe cried out to him from the bottom of the hill.

"Hey, you there! Get out of the way! We're doing a take!"

Vincent strained to hear what the young fool was saying to him.

"A take? A take? What's he blabbering on about?"

Without warning, Wayne and O'Hara came flying around the corner on the bike. Quinn grabbed Vincent by the sleeve and yanked him back onto the pavement as the tandem missed him by a hair's breadth. Vincent jerked his arm out of Quinn's grip without a word of thanks. Quinn shook his head and walked away. Joe called out down the road once more.

"Sir. Please. If you could just stay where you are for the moment. We're going for one more take."

Vincent hollered back up the street.

"One more take? Not with me it won't be, you blasted Hollywood hooligans."

As he directed his rage in the general direction of Joe and the crew, Wayne and O'Hara walked past him back towards the market cross.

"Take it easy, mister," drawled Wayne. "It's only a movie."

"Well, Mr Duke," sneered Vincent as the two actors continued on their way, "this is one 'movie' I won't be paying good money to see, you can be sure of that, you bunch of idle-rich layabouts."

Wayne and O'Hara ignored the old man as he threw a few more choice words in their direction before disappearing into Hanratty's.

An agitated Vincent approached the bar to order a drink. The place was deserted. Not a single customer. Behind the bar sat

Peter, the elder brother of the proprietor, Sean Hanratty. He puffed on his pipe in a world of his own, oblivious to Vincent's presence. Vincent slapped the bar in exasperation.

"Service. A pint, if you please."

Sean Hanratty emerged through the door behind the bar carrying an open bottle of whisky in one hand and a glass in the other. He was in his late-fifties, a thin rodent-like man with a widow's peak, watery eyes and a permanent five o'clock shadow. He wore a grubby apron over a black waistcoat, with his shirtsleeves rolled up to reveal his thin arms. A carbon-copy of his brother Peter, minus the pipe.

"So. Been converted on the road to Damascus, have we?" said Sean.

"Ryan's Bar not good enough for you any more, I suppose?"

Vincent surveyed the yawning emptiness of the pub.

"Seems to me you need all the converts you can get. If you're going to break a habit of a lifetime and be discriminating of your clientele, then I'll take my custom elsewhere."

Sean put down his drink and started to pull a pint of beer for his one and only customer.

"Well then," said Sean, forcing his thin lips to pursue a jolly smile. "Long time no see, Vincent, me boy. In fact long time never see come to that," he said, laughing at his own very bad joke.

"How have you been keeping?" Vincent conjured up a

phlegm-riddled cough accompanied by a theatrical gasp for breath, indicating he was not long for this world as he patted his chest.

"It's the rheumy. Damp days and cold nights. I'm not as young as I used to be," said Vincent, as he reached for the beer. "Cheers."

He picked up the glass with one hand and dropped four pennies on the bar with the other. Peter moved for the first time, leaning forward on his stool as Sean stared at the money. The younger brother proffered Vincent a questioning look. Vincent returned the stare with equal intensity. Peter snorted a nose full of pipe smoke then leant back against the wall.

"What's that?" demanded Sean, pointing to the coins in front of him.

"What do you mean? I'm paying you for my drink," Vincent retorted. "That's what that is. Don't worry, Catholics trade in the same coinage as you lot."

Sean and Peter both jerked their thumbs at the same time back towards a chalk board on the wall behind them above the optics, exactly the same as the one in Ryan's Bar.

"You see that? Fivepence ha'penny a pint."

Vincent slammed his glass on the bar.

"Jesus Mary Mother of Christ! Not you as well? Where in the name of God around here is a decent man going to be able to pay a decent price for a decent pint of beer? You're all a bunch of blood-suckers, that's what you are. Leeches. Every single bar in this village the same. I've a good mind to shop the lot of you to the Weights and Measures men, so help me I am."

Sean Hanratty leaned over the bar.

"And they'd be more than happy to pay a call upon you one cold night and inspect your still, no doubt, Mr Vincent Unlicensed-Poteen-Seller Corrigan."

Vincent angrily swallowed his pint in one gulp, then cracked the glass down hard on the counter. Without saying a word he took back the four pennies, reached into his pocket and counted out the money he owed for the drink in farthings and ha'pennies.

The brothers watched in silence while Vincent fumed on the other side of the bar. He tossed the final farthing onto the counter and watched as it rolled across the bar and onto the floor. Peter jumped from his stool with the agility of a man half his age, and retrieved the money. Placing the coin in his trouser pocket he sat back on the stool, puffing on his pipe and staring off into the distance like a stone statue.

Vincent got to the door then turned to face Sean Hanratty.

"Swindling Protestant!" Vincent bawled before slamming the door behind him.

CHAPTER THREE

In any small community news travels fast, and Cong was no exception. Before the afternoon was out the whole village knew that Patrick O'Dea had returned to the fold. Details of how he had casually strolled into Ryan's Bar and ordered a drink as if he'd never been gone were also being circulated. Along with the fact that he'd eluded payment of his round as well.

All this was being discussed in almost every household within Cong while Patrick still sat in the bar cadging drinks from Dunphy with the promise of paying once he'd got himself employment on the film. Every household except, that is, the O'Dea's.

Mary had gone to Spiddal to visit her sister, and Heather had tagged along for diplomatic reasons, rather than any emotional attachment towards her aunt. Her mother's sister resembled Mary too much for Heather to be anything but cordial and polite when spoken to. Which wasn't very often once the sisters started gabbing away.

Heather had spent the day in the company of her mother in the hope that when it came time to announce her intention to attend the village dance, Mary would look upon it in a more positive light. Which is why at 8 o'clock that evening Heather walked into the parlour dressed for her date with Joe, fully expecting only token resistance from her mother. It took approximately thirty seconds for her to find out she had underestimated Mary and her proclivity to think the worst of any situation. Particularly when it concerned her children.

She stood in the doorway leading into the parlour, and watched her mother sitting in her favourite chair by the empty fireside sewing a pair of Thomas's trousers.

"That brother of yours has some explaining to do," said Mary as she sensed Heather entering the room. "Tea was over an hour ago and he hasn't even bothered..." She turned to see her daughter standing in the middle of the room and dropped her sewing. Heather wore a flowered skirt and a white blouse with a scarf around her neck. It took a few seconds for Mary to register that it was actually her daughter stood in front of her.

"What are you dressed like that for?" asked Mary as if she were talking to a child. Heather took a deep breath and walked across the room to face a mirror above the sideboard. She teased her still damp hair with her fingers as she talked to her mother's reflection.

"I'm going to the village hall," she said. "There's a gathering there tonight, a dance of some sort. The film company organised it. Wasn't that nice of them?"

"No daughter of mine is going out unaccompanied on a Saturday night, and I'm certainly not taking you."

"Fine," replied Heather, turning to face her mother. "I'll go on my own then."

"Get upstairs and dress yourself properly. You're not going anywhere and that's final."

Mary silently resumed her sewing.

Heather tried to control the thick feeling of frustration that grew inside her for fear she might say something they would both regret. But the years of being shouted down by her mother had taken their toll.

"Mother, you listen to me now. I didn't tell you I was going out before because I knew you'd make a fuss. But I'm 18 years old, and I can look after myself now."

Mary stood and approached her daughter.

"You wouldn't talk to me like that if your father were here. Your father..." Heather cut her off. She'd heard these lines before.

"Well he's not here and I'm going and that's an end to it," she said.

Mary stiffened then uttered something that was just barely audible to Heather.

"What did you say?"

Mary returned to her chair and picked up the trousers she had been sewing. Heather planted herself in front of the chair and leaned over her.

"I said what did you say?"

Mary looked into her daughter's eyes with a coldly defiant

glare.

"I said you looked cheap."

Heather caught her breath, turned and made for the door.

"And you're nothing but a mean, bitter twisted old woman. No wonder he left."

She slammed the door behind her. Heather composed herself outside the house, taking several deep breaths before deciding she was calm enough for the evening ahead. And God help Joe Yates if he says anything out of turn, she swore to herself, deliberating on what she might do to him within the bounds of the law should he take it into his head to try any of that 'funny stuff' he had referred to the day before.

Highly strung and emotionally charged, Heather vacated the doorstep outside her house and stormed off to meet an unsuspecting Joe Yates.

Heather's departure was fortunate for Patrick O'Dea, who turned up not less than a minute later from the other direction. He was tired and emotional from having spent the whole afternoon in the company of Michael Dunphy, and anybody else who could be cajoled into buying him a drink. Thomas held his father up as best he could, leaning him against the wall with a huge sigh of relief. Patrick winked at his son and pulled him close, speaking in a half-whisper.

"Remember, Tommy boy, don't let on to your mother we've

been at Ryan's. You know she doesn't like me drinking. Will you do for that me, little feller?"

Thomas nodded. A blind man could have seen his father was drunk and knew the prospect of a happy reunion in the next few minutes was as about as remote as a man walking on the moon. Deciding not to delay the inevitable Thomas slowly opened the front door, then helped his father across the step into the house. He chose to stay outside as he pulled the door shut behind his father then sat down on the step, listening with his ear to the door. He heard his mother speak first.

"Thomas, where the devil have you..." followed by an ominous silence, the shock almost palpable from where Thomas sat. He jumped as Mary let out a shriek then a series of muffled words consisting of his father's name being repeated over and over again.

"Oh, Patrick, you've come back to me," he could hear her sobbing, his father either too overwhelmed or too inebriated to respond in kind. Thomas was just about to join the happy couple in the happy household when a sound he knew all too well cracked through the air like the snap of a whip as his mother's hand made contact with the side of Patrick's face.

"That's for being down at Ryan's, I can smell it on your stinking breath and this..." Another slap. Thomas closed the door and sat back down on the step. "...is for leaving me and the children all alone for the last two years while you drank your way around Ireland, you good for nothing drunken little swine!"

Thomas smiled to himself. His father had come back at last and now it was just like the old days again. And right at that moment, despite the bickering and slapping that went on in the house behind him, Thomas wouldn't have wanted it any other way.

The frantic duelling of flute and fiddle drifting through the air from the direction of the village hall gave the impression that the dancing was in full swing. Once inside, however, those who had been attracted by the sound of the music were disappointed to say the least. Quinn and his fellow musicians played their canon of traditional music for all they were worth but nobody appeared to want to break the ice and get the party going.

Joe and the rest of the film crew stood to one side of the hall helping themselves to generous cups of punch spiked with whiskey. A contingent of local boys from the surrounding community had stationed themselves on the other side of the hall, ingesting large quantities of their own home made beer and what appeared to be white spirits of a highly questionable nature.

In between these two groups sat Gallagher and Father Donnelly, tapping their feet along to the music. Reverend

Casey was conspicuous by his absence.

A fourth group consisting entirely of girls from in and around the village sat with their backs firmly against the wall, avoiding any inclination to allow their gaze to wander across the hall in the direction of the local boys. Not one of them was prepared to initiate eye contact with any of the boys for fear their reputation would be ruined before the night was out, and be named as the outrageous flirt known to all in County Mayo, County Sligo, Connemara and all surrounding areas by first light the following day.

An impatient, anxious, nervous Joe whispered to Gene as he eyed the door.

"Do you think she'll come?" said Joe, not really wanting to hear what Gene thought just in case he gave the wrong answer. Gene placed a paternal hand on the young man's shoulder.

"She'll be here, don't you worry," replied Gene.

"You think so? Really?" said Joe, happy that Gene was so sure.

"Joe, quit worrying. It's only just gone eight." he said studying his wristwatch.

"There's plenty of time."

A boisterous group of teenage boys were gathered on the opposite side of the hall. One of them in particular, a young man with extremely large hands, and a face full of stubble, looked to the casual onlooker as though he and trouble were kindred spirits.

"Anyway," said Gene, "I have a feeling your date not turning up tonight is going to be the least of our troub..." An excited Joe suddenly grabbed Gene by the arm.

"There she is! Look!"

Heather walked slowly and self consciously into the hall, looked around to locate Joe, then gave him a nervous little wave before walking over to join the group of girls fixed to the wall. Joe's heart leapt at the sight of Heather, now absolutely convinced that she was the most beautiful girl in the village. In fact he was so elated by the mere fact that Heather had actually shown up that he failed to register how she now ignored him from the other side of the hall. The unshaven teenager watched Heather at the same time, his eyes narrowing to small black lines above his stubble as he saw her wave to Joe.

"Did you see that? Did you see that?" Joe jabbered to Gene. "She waved. She waved to me." They were joined by Bo who had left the vicinity of the punch bowl with a look of disgust having gauged the alcoholic ineffectiveness of the dark purple liquid within.

"She waved?" said Bo. "She waved and you're standing there as if the Lakers have just lost the World Series? What are you, nuts?"

"What do you mean?" said Joe with a hurtful frown.

"What he means is are you two gonna spend all evening just jerking your arms at each other across the hall all evening? Me and Bo and the guys go to all this trouble to arrange a dance and set you up with the girl of your dreams and all you're gonna do is wave?"

"What are you talking about *go to all this trouble*? The old man said it would be a good idea to throw this dance and I think it is. I happen to agree with the miserable old coot for once, but don't go telling me this is all for my benefit."

"If the old man thinks it's such a great idea, how come he ain't here, huh?" countered Gene. Joe shrugged.

"How should I know? Maybe he's got something better to do. Like making a movie."

Gene was about to answer Joe when Gallagher approached and shook Gene by the hand.

"It's a fine thing you've done here tonight, Mr Willis, a fine thing. Much appreciated, I'm sure."

"No problem, sir, just thought we'd lay on a little entertainment for all those people who've been so kind to us since we came here. Isn't that right, Bo?"

The four of them turned as one and observed the disparate groups of isolated people spaced around the hall. Gallagher nodded.

"Give them some time, Mr Willis. The evening is still quite

young as they say. Drink?"

Much to Gene's surprise and Bo's delight, Gallagher pulled out a bottle of whisky he had concealed inside his jacket. Bo took him by the arm and hurriedly led him towards the punch bowl. Gene started to follow them then turned back to Joe who stood staring across the hall at Heather.

"If you don't ask her to dance, Mr Yates, I will personally inform the old man you'd rather work with Howard Hawks anytime."

The thought of Ford on his back again galvanised Joe into action. He glanced over to where Heather stood talking and laughing with her friends and caught her throwing a sly glance in his direction. He grabbed two glasses and filled them with punch. The boy with the stubble moved next to Joe and glared at him. Not realising that he was the target of intimidation, Joe began the long walk towards Heather, across the hall. A hall that now appeared to be more than forty miles long and twenty miles wide.

Joe suddenly felt someone trip him up. He tried to regain his balance, failed, and tumbled to the floor. He lay in a pool of punch as his attacker stood above him surrounded by his laughing friends and cronies. Joe's first thought was to wonder if Heather had witnessed his ignominy at the hands of the unknown teenager.

The music stopped as Joe staggered to his feet, shaking the

drops of punch from his wet hands.

"You okay?" asked Gene. Joe brushed his trousers and rubbed his knee.

"Yeah, I guess so," replied Joe looking back at the grinning boy. Gene put his hand on Joe's shoulder.

"Come on, I'll go back to the castle with you, get you cleaned up."

Joe brushed Gene's hand away.

"No, I'm alright." Joe's evening had been ruined before it had even started. He wanted to be somewhere, anywhere, just as long as it was as far away from this place as possible.

"I'm going. I'm... I just... I'm okay but..."

Joe turned and walked from the hall without a backward glance.

He was furious, or as furious as he could get anyway. It wasn't as furious as some others could be, his anger not able to hold a candle to the likes of Ford, or John Wayne for that matter, when it came to flying off the handle. But he was mad. Angry and mad enough to ignore Heather as she called out to him. He continued to walk away as her voice trailed him down the street.

"Joe, Joe. Wait. Wait a minute." Joe's step faltered momentarily, but his embarrassment drove him on. Heather stopped running and stood in the middle of the road as he walked towards Ashford Castle.

"Joseph Yates! You stop right there this minute!"

This was not an impassioned plea, it was a direct order and Joe did what he always did when faced with the voice of authority. He obeyed, rooted to the spot as Heather walked towards him.

"And where do you think you're going? I didn't get all dressed up tonight so I could be stood up by the likes of you."

Joe turned to confront her, his anger still at boiling point.

"Stood up? You barely acknowledged my presence in there. Just a little wave..." Joe mimicked with a flutter of his hand. "... then that guy in there – who was that guy anyway?"

"His name's Michael Cassidy. Or as me and most of my friends refer to him, "the village idiot"."

Joe's voice jumped a register at the painful memory of a few moments before. "Well, he sure made me look like some kind of a fool."

Joe wasn't an expert in the behavioural habits of the female of the species, but he knew enough to know Heather was not about to feel pity for him. She didn't let him down.

"So what did you want me to do, Mr Yates? Throw myself into your loving arms the minute I walked into the hall? Make a fool of myself instead?"

Joe shut his eyes and tilted his head skywards. He didn't want to argue. That had been the last thing on his mind. What would John Wayne have done, he thought to himself. What did Wayne's character do when Maureen O'Hara chastised him in the scene they filmed the other day? He stayed calm but remained strong. He didn't let her win the argument but he stayed calm. Joe decided to stay calm. But strong.

"Of course I didn't want you to throw yourself at me. It's only I kind of feel you could have done more than just wave, that's all."

They both turned around and looked back down the street towards the hall as the music suddenly became louder, the evening air echoing with the sound of clapping and whooping from the people inside.

Heather smiled.

"Sounds like everybody's finally enjoying themselves," she said.

Heather's subdued voice caused Joe to relax for the first time since more than five hours before she had turned up at the hall. Who knows, he prayed to himself, maybe something might still be salvaged from the wreckage of the evening.

"Yeah. All it took was for somebody to break the ice. Me."

Heather smiled then took Joe by the arm.

"Let's go for a walk."

Back at the hall Gallagher sat with Gene and Bo as they did their best to deplete the contents of Gallagher's whisky bottle in the quickest possible time. All three of them felt puffed out from their exertions on the dance floor, Gallagher more so than the others. He unbuttoned the top of his shirt, raised a glass to his new friends then leaned closer to Gene so that he could be heard above the loud playing of the band.

"So, Mr Willis, would you be knowing Miss O'Hara on a more personal basis, if you get my drift?"

Gallagher noted the caution in Gene's voice a she replied, "What do you mean, on a more personal basis?"

From the look on Gene's face Gallagher realised that his remark had been misconstrued. He shook his head.

"No, no, no, Mr Willis, I wasn't for one minute suggesting - God forbid - I was just asking whether or not... Oh, Jesus I've gone and done it now. I was just asking..."

"...if I know Maureen O'Hara very well, is that it?" interrupted Gene.

Gallagher nodded.

"I couldn't have put it better, Mr Willis. In fact, I didn't."

"Call me Gene, Mr Gallagher. I know Miss O'Hara well, we've worked together on a couple of films. As a matter of fact she was in the last movie Mr Ford made back in the

States, Rio Grande. Have you seen it yet?"

Gallagher shook his head, which was warm and sweating.

"I haven't as yet, but I'm sure Miss O'Hara is as beautiful to look at in that one as she is in all her films."

"Yes, she's a fine looking woman, Mr Gallagher."

Bo poured out the rest of the precious drink.

"Dermot. The name's Dermot." He raised his glass. "To Miss O'Hara." The others joined him, raising their glasses in a toast to the actress. Gallagher took a large swallow then moved closer to Gene.

"I was thinking, Gene, might it be possible to meet - in company of course - with Miss O'Hara sometime when she's not too busy? If it wouldn't be too inconvenient at a later stage in the not too distant future. Work permitting and all that."

"Well, Dermot," said Gene, putting a friendly hand on Gallagher's shoulder. "I'm afraid I have some bad news for you. You see, Miss O'Hara isn't strictly speaking a Miss. She's a Mrs. And she has a seven-year-old daughter to prove it."

Gallagher fought to hide his disappointment, his whole life now officially declared futile and meaningless in the space of a few seconds.

"You will be able to meet her in person, though," Gene said. The light returned to Gallagher's eyes.

"At the garden fete tomorrow afternoon. I think Wayne, Ford and Miss O'Hara intend to put in some kind of appearance. I'll check it out for you and let you know in the morning. Okay?"

Gallagher raised the glass to his lips with an unsteady hand.

"A true gentleman, Gene, a true gentleman."

Gene sank his drink in one go.

"I do my best."

The music from the hall faded into the distance as Heather and Joe made their way down the street. They paused at the bridge that spanned the River Cong. On one side of the bridge itself was a small cottage covered in a swirl of plants and flowers. The scent of roses and clematis competed for the senses of those who wandered past.

Joe pointed to the cottage.

"That's the priest's house in the movie. We film him and the bishop coming out of the front door, then match it with a shot of the wall outside Ashford Castle to make it look as though they're one and the same place. Clever, huh?"

They walked on to the bridge and leaned over the wall, looking down into the darkness below. Three globes of light danced and shimmered upon the surface of the water.

"Your film's not the only illusion," Heather said. "Look."

She pointed to the light on the left.

"This one is obviously from the lamp at the end of the bridge down there. That's the lamp just above us. And the one in the middle..." Heather pointed to the sky. "That's the moon. You think it's a light but it's not. It's the moon."

Joe looked up at the sky.

"It does no harm," he said in a half-whisper. "Illusion, I mean.

We're not fooling the audience, we're just taking liberties with reality. Nobody gets hurt. Do they?"

He hoped his reply had not upset her. Heather gave a little shrug.

"I guess not. I just think people will look at your film and see an Ireland that doesn't really exist, that's all. An Ireland that is as much a figment of your imagination..."

"Ford's imagination, Heather. Not mine. Okay?" Heather smiled.

"Alright, an Ireland that comes from the imagination of Mr Ford. Either way, it doesn't exist, your Mr Ford's Ireland. It's going to look very pretty once it's up there on the screen, I'm sure of that, but it's not the real thing."

This time it was Joe's turn to shrug.

"Heather, there's a whole industry in Hollywood that does nothing but make things up for a paying audience. They've been doing it for years. Get a lot of money out of it too. And I could think of worse ways of making a living, believe me."

Heather nodded her head in a passable gesture of agreement.

"I'll defer judgement until I've seen the film. Agreed?"

"Agreed," said Joe, his heart scraping a hole through his chest as Heather's fingers caressed his hand. They turned to each other.

"Do you like it here?" asked Heather.

"Here? Cong, you mean?"

"Cong, Connemara, Ireland."

Joe struggled to find the right words. But as usual they didn't come easy as he looked up at the night sky for inspiration.

"Well, let me see... er... the scenery... it's... well it's like something out of a film and the ladies..." He glanced down at Heather. "And the ladies, they're just fine. Real fine."

Heather moved closer.

"Is that all? Just 'fine'?"

Joe shut his eyes and clenched his empty hand.

"Why is it that whenever I'm around you I never seem to be able to say the right thing?"

"You'll improve. You just need to get in some practise, that's all."

Joe opened his eyes and looked at Heather, her face bathed in the radiant glow from the lamp above.

"You look like an angel."

"It's the light playing tricks. An illusion."

Joe put his arm around Heather's waist and pressed his body against her.

"No. No Hollywood lights here."

Joe lowered his lips onto Heather's mouth, wanting to savour every second of their first kiss. Heather responded in kind, both of them luxuriating in the passion of the moment.

After an eternity they let go of each other. Joe looked at Heather as she stood with her eyes still closed and head tilted towards the light and knew that as long as he lived he would never see anything as beautiful again. Heather smiled.

"Do that again."

Joe looked around in a mild panic, realising for the first time that somebody might be watching them. Ford had drummed into the crew time and time again not to fraternise with the community on pain of death. Joe took this warning very seriously indeed, his mouth drying in fear at the thought of what Ford might do to him if he found out. He let go of Heather and stepped away.

"Uh, don't you think we should be getting back to the hall? I mean, people might… you know… We've been out here for quite a while and…"

Heather laughed and grabbed Joe by the hand, leading him back towards the hall.

"Come on, then. Let's just hope you dance better than you kiss."

By the time Joe and Heather got back to the hall the party was in full swing and nobody paid them a blind bit of notice.

Dancers promenaded back and forth across the floor in time to the band as Quinn clapped and called out the steps. Gene partnered one of Heather's friends, Kathy Donahue, and as they passed in front of Joe and Heather Gene pulled both of them onto the floor. Joe skipped for a moment or two before picking up on the rhythm of the music, then danced as smoothly as his gangly body would allow. He beamed down at Heather, happy in the knowledge that he could put his arms around her without fear of being castigated. Even the presence of a near comatose Cassidy was not enough to wipe the smile from Joe's face as he twirled Heather around the dance hall.

After dancing non-stop for almost half an hour, a breathless Heather took Joe to the doorway and, standing on tip-toe, shouted into his ear in order to be heard above the music.

"I'm sorry, Joe but I have to go now. I'd love to stay longer but..."

Joe looked at his watch. It was nearly nine-thirty. Where had the time gone?

"But why?" he asked, his heart sinking. What had he done now?

"My mother will be wondering where I am."

"Does your mother always need to know where you are?"

She seemed shocked.

"Of course. You never know who you might stumble into in the middle of the night around here."

"Or over," mumbled Joe, looking at Cassidy who now sat slumped against the wall, dead to the world at large.

"Never mind him. He's no trouble to you, not in that state. Just ignore him."

Joe took Heather by the hand.

"Can I walk you home?"

She shook her head.

"You'd better not. I'm just getting my mother used to the fact that I want to go out on my own. If she sees me with you there'll be hell to pay."

"How do I get to see you again?"

Heather jumped up and kissed him lightly on the cheek.

"You'll think of something."

Joe followed her out of the hall and watched her walk down the road towards her house. She turned and waved. Joe returned the wave as a slightly inebriated and quite breathless Gene stood next to him, leaning on the younger man for support.

"There you go with all that goddam waving again. Come on, let's have a drink."

He pulled him back inside whilst Joe strained to catch one last glimpse of Heather as she disappeared from beneath the light of the gas lamp at the end of the street.

Heather stood outside the house, took a deep breath and braced herself for the inevitable confrontation with her mother. No light shone through the front window from the parlour, which meant that either Mary had gone to bed early with one of her heads or, with a bit of luck, she was round Mildred Grady's house bending her ear with stories of how her wayward daughter had dragged the family name through the dirt.

Either way, Heather was not in the mood for arguing. This was her night, hers and Joe's. Nobody was going to take it away from her.

She opened the door and tiptoed into the parlour, locating a small paraffin lamp on the window sill. Lighting the lamp Heather trod as lightly as possible as she made her way up the stairs. Despite the gentleness of her step the wood still creaked and moved beneath her feet.

As she reached the top of the stairs Heather could have sworn she heard heavy snoring coming from her mother's room. It must be her hearing playing tricks on her after the loudness of the music in the hall. But the snoring persisted.

She crept to the door and listened, confused by the noise. Her mother never snored and had slept alone since the night her father had left. The only conclusion was that Mary was indeed the source. Turning away to walk down the corridor to her own bedroom she caught a slight movement to her left, and saw Thomas peeking from behind his bedroom door. He beckoned her into his room.

Heather sat on the end of her brother's bed as he clambered beneath the covers and reached over to place the lamp on the bedside table.

"Da came back today," Thomas whispered.

Heather nearly dropped the lamp as a raft of differing emotions coursed through her body. Anger, despair, bewilderment, curiosity and a surprise feeling of happiness all rushed together at the same instant making Heather dizzier than she had been when Joe had swung her around the dance floor not more than ten minutes before.

Then she remembered how her father had left without a word, leaving her and Thomas to mop up the hurt their mother had felt at being abandoned, and anger won through.

"He's back?" she screeched. "He runs to God knows where for two years then waltzes back here like he's never been away? The impudence of the man, the sheer bloody..."

Thomas put his hand over Heather's mouth to quieten her.

"At least he's back alive, Heather," said Thomas quietly.

She pushed his hand away.

"Not for long. I'm going to kill him," she whispered, the shadow of her hands looming large on the wall as she mimed the act of strangulation. "With my bare hands, so help me, I'll..."

"Heather, be quiet. Don't wake them, not now, please. Not when ma's so happy."

Heather caught the urgency in Thomas's voice, and dropped her hands to her lap.

If her mother was happy lying next to a drunken irresponsible wanderer whose snoring was getting louder by the minute, then the moment Joe proposed to her, as she knew he surely would, then she would be off. Out and away from Cong quicker than her feet could carry her.

She might not even bother saying goodbye, Heather thought to herself, seeing as it was something of a family trait not to let on when moving to pastures green. Of course, she'd let Thomas know, getting up from the bed and ruffling her brother's hair before picking up the lamp and walking over to the door.

"Don't worry, Tommy, I won't wake them. But take my word for it, tonight will be the last peaceful night in this house for a very long time, you can be sure of that."

Heather went to her bedroom, her mind full of her father and Joe. Even the unexpected presence of a wayward parent in the house did nothing to dampen her enthusiasm for the shy young man from Hollywood. In fact it positively encouraged it.

As she slid beneath the blanket she thought to herself that her father's surprise homecoming might actually be a blessing in disguise. Maybe there was use for the drunken fool yet.

CHAPTER FOUR

The morning mist still hovered above the ground as Gerald O'Brien stole across the field behind his house. From a distance anyone watching might think he looked about a foot shorter with the lower half of his legs hidden beneath the swirling clouds of fog. An ancient stone wall lay at the end of O'Brien's field separating his land from the main road. Peering over the top of the wall he looked to his left and then his right, in case anyone should suddenly appear.

Not that there was much hope of that at 6:30 on a Sunday morning, but O'Brien had his reasons for not wanting to be seen. For this was the morning he would initiate his plan and strike a blow of freedom for the common man. No faceless bureaucratic entity called the ESB was going to get the better of him, he would make sure of that. Boone and his cronies would pay for not sticking to their original agreement, an agreement that would have put enough money in O'Brien's pocket to see him straight for the rest of his life.

No matter that Boone never actually agreed to anything in the first place. It was of no consequence to him, O'Brien, that he was the one who had pushed Boone on the matter of compensation for allowing the ESB to plant electricity poles on his land.

Boone had strung him along just for the sake of a quiet life, knowing right from the beginning that the ESB had no funds put aside to remunerate inconvenienced landowners. To O'Brien's wounded pride, however, it was a matter of principle. He had done Boone and the ESB a favour in allowing them access to his land, and now he wanted something in return. O'Brien felt morally obliged to remind those who reneged on a deal the consequences of their actions. And remind them in a big way.

On the other side of the road stood a lorry with a large drum of black cable on the back. The ESB had laid the cables and the poles along the side of the road leading into Cong, leaving their equipment unattended at night, aware that in a remote and rural area like County Mayo there wouldn't be much call for cable and diggers.

Which was just what O'Brien had planned on.

Creeping across the road he opened the lorry door and reached across towards a wooden box located between the driver and passenger seat. He lifted the lid to reveal three small bundles of red sticks with *DYNAMITE* written in large black letters down the side of each batch. O'Brien placed two of the bundles in the inside pocket of his jacket then retreated across the field, covering over his footsteps as best he could.

He reached the warmth of his house safe in the knowledge that if the crew working for the ESB were as stupid as Boone then they'd never miss a thing.

If, on the other hand, they noticed the dynamite was missing they'd never trace it to his house.

Because the second part of the grand plan was to find some idiot to hide it for him.

Breakfast in the dining hall at Ashford Castle later the following morning began, fortunately for Joe, Gene and Bo, as a slightly muted affair. Fortunate because yet again their heads had taken the full weight of punishment due to them through the ingestion of large quantities of alcohol the night before. For the second day running all three felt and in fact looked older than John Ford and John Wayne combined, if such a thing were possible.

Ford chewed on a piece of bread as Maureen O'Hara left the table to take her young daughter for a walk in the early morning sun. A chuckling Wayne poured the three budding alcoholics a cup of coffee each.

"Take my advice from somebody who knows, Joe. You make a habit of hanging around with these guys in the evening and they'll be shipping you back in a wooden box. Ain't that right, Pappy?" he turned to Ford, who nodded.

"By the way, me and Pappy were discussing the fight sequence yesterday and..."

Ford turned to Joe.

"Fetch the bowl."

Joe reached across behind him and retrieved a small wooden

bowl from one of the other tables. Wayne reached into his pocket and pulled out a pound note. Ford took it from him and placed it in the bowl.

Wayne threw his hands in the air.

"Hey, it's usually fifty cents!"

"You got fifty cents on you, Duke?"

"No, I don't have fifty cents on me, on account I ain't got no American money. You know that," said Wayne.

"Then until you get fifty cents it's going to cost an Irish pound every time you or anybody else brings up the subject of the film, or any of my films for that matter, at the breakfast table. You know the rules, Duke. No talking shop."

Wayne pointed to the bowl containing his confiscated pound note.

"I figure that money buys me an awful lot of shop talk. Agreed?"

Ford shrugged.

"Agreed."

"Okay, then," said Wayne, turning to Gene and Bo. "Pappy here says we're gonna need a few more extras when we shoot the final sequence for the fight down at the farm this week. Gene, I thought maybe you could put some kind of notice in one of the shops in the main street telling everybody we're looking for extras. Might be we could raise a few this afternoon down at the church."

Gene nodded slowly so as not to disturb the finely balanced pain behind his forehead. Joe threw back his coffee and for a few seconds felt human once more.

"Say, Duke," offered Joe, "if you want I can organise putting together a list of names or something."

"Sounds good to me."

Ford held out the bowl to Joe and shook it in front of his face. Joe stared at him.

"Fifty cents, son," Ford said. Joe reached reluctantly into his pocket, knowing he wasn't going to be able to get away with less than a pound, but he was in no mood for arguing, especially with Ford.

Wayne grabbed the bowl from the director, handed Joe's pound back to him and threw in another pound note of his own.

"This one's on me, Joe."

Wayne left the table, quickly followed by Joe, Gene and Bo. The minute they left the room Ford rolled the notes up and put them in his pocket, grinning to himself. He sat back and lit his pipe, knowing he had successfully managed to rile Wayne yet again. And the day had hardly begun.

Breakfast in the O'Dea household promised to be anything but muted, mainly because it was the first time the whole family had gathered around the same table since Patrick had taken off. To Heather's muted fury, the fact that he had returned with his tail between his legs did nothing to negate Patrick's assumed divine right as head of the household once more. Heather had entered the kitchen to find her father, wearing a pair of old trousers and a vest, sat at the end of the table, a position she had occupied in his absence. Patrick had his back to her as he called out to Thomas in the kitchen.

"Thomas, where's the butter I asked for? This bread's going stale with the waiting." Heather slammed the door shut behind her and sat opposite him with her arms folded, not saying a word. Thomas brought in the butter then ran back into the kitchen. Mary walked into the parlour with a tray of tea, humming rather too loudly for comfort. Patrick watched as Mary poured him a cup of tea. She then held the tea pot towards Heather but her daughter ignored her. Mary left the room for the safety of the kitchen. After a while Patrick finally made eye contact with Heather.

"So. You've grown I see,"

Heather nodded silently.

"Got yourself a feller yet?"

Heather shrugged.

"No one special," she said, keeping her voice even and steady. Patrick visibly relaxed. Heather knew that she could pounce on her father at any moment now that his defences were down, spit venom and contempt in his direction until he withered and melted beneath the onslaught of pent up anger and fury that boiled inside her.

Heather decided that was not to be her way, not yet at any rate. She would bide her time safe in the knowledge that now he had returned she would be free to leave the village at the drop of a hat. Preferably Joe's hat if she had anything to do with it, but either way she was not going to hang around for much longer.

Her main concern was that if she didn't control herself and let her father know what she really thought of him, it might encourage him to run off again and that was something she wished to avoid at all costs. She reached across the table and picked up the tea pot.

"More tea, father?"

Despite having been overwhelmed with joy at his father's return, Thomas got out of the house as fast as he could, not wanting to endure the tension any more than he had to. He joined up with his friends Billy and Michael down by the stream, the three of them playing cowboys and Indians for most of the morning in the woods nearby. Thomas insisted on being the sheriff with Michael as his faithful sidekick. As usual it fell to Billy to be the pesky Indian varmint, a role he had honed to near perfection, especially when it came to the act of dying.

Nobody died as spectacularly as Billy McGee, launching himself out of the undergrowth and twitching in mid air as the bullets slammed into his body, rolling over and over down the grass slope at the edge of the woods until coming to rest with his head hanging over the small bank of the stream. Michael slumped against a tree with an arrow in his shoulder, but Thomas remained unharmed, blowing smoke from the end of his imaginary gun barrel while Billy's body ripened in the late morning sun.

On their way back for dinner the three of them turned the corner into the main street to see a small crowd of people jostling to get a glimpse of a notice placed in the window of the post office. Thomas pulled his friends to one side and took command of the situation.

"Billy, get down on your hands and knees and crawl through their legs. Take a look and see what all the fuss is about."

Billy dutifully dropped on all fours and snaked his way beneath the crowd.

After a moment or two Thomas and Michael saw a tiny hand emerge from between the legs of one of the onlookers. Grabbing Billy by the arm they pulled him from the pile of tangled limbs that seemed to be growing by the minute.

"Well?" Thomas and Michael asked at the same time.

"They're looking at some kind of notice stuck on the window."

Thomas sighed and looked at Michael.

"We can see that," said Thomas. "What does the note say?"

"How should I know?" shrugged Billy. "I can't read."

"Wait here," said Michael, pushing both of them out of the way as he squeezed himself into the packed bodies. He emerged a moment later, fighting for breath as the three of them ran down the road.

"They need a whole crowd of extras for a fight they want to film over by Ashford farm. And anybody can apply!"

"Anyone? You, me? Does that mean we can all be in the film then?" asked a highly excited Thomas.

"I don't see why not," replied Michael. "Hey, Billy, tell him how much your brother got for being an extra the other day."

"One pound and six shillings. A day!"

Thomas's mouth popped open like a dead fish.

"A day? No. I don't believe you." Billy nodded.

"It's true, God's honest. And not only that, they fed him as well. And they want him back for another whole week too. He said he eats better on the film than he does at home."

"One pound six shillings a day," exclaimed Thomas. "Jesus."

Thomas yelped in pain as Gerald O'Brien appeared from nowhere and clipped him round the ear.

"Language, you little bleeder," spat O'Brien.

Thomas hissed in pain, contemplated running after the idiot O'Brien and booting him up the arse then thought better of it.

He'd tell his da instead.

"When are they going to choose the extras?" he asked Michael.

"At the fête this afternoon, over by the church. You know. The one for Cruelty to Children."

"Is that for or against, do you think?" asked Thomas, still rubbing his ear. The boys reached the bottom of the street and started to walk off towards their respective homes in time for dinner. Michael called out to the other two as he went.

"See you this afternoon then. About three?"

"Too right," said Billy, running off back to his house. Thomas's previous excitement at the possibility of actually appearing in a film with John Wayne was tempered by the thought of what his mother would say. Now that he was yards from his house reality dawned.

"Nah, I don't think I'll be able to make it," he called out.

Michael shouted back from a few houses down.

"Come on. "I heard somebody say John Wayne might even be there himself. Don't you want to be in the film?"

"Of course I do but I know what me ma will say. She's already said I'm not to mix with those Hollywood types. Says I'll be..."

Thomas thought for a moment as he tried to recall the exact words his mother had uttered to him at least once a day since the film crew had arrived in the village.

"She said something about corruption, I think it was,

whatever that might be, material wealth, spiritual indecency and someone called Mammon."

Michael's look of bewilderment said it all.

"I know," said Thomas. "`I don't know what it means either."

"`Forget what your ma says. My da never listens to a word my ma says because he's the man of the house. You've been the man of the house while your da's been away so you should be doing what you want to do whenever you want to do it."

Thomas tried to follow the logic of Michael's fragmented thought process only to come to the inevitable conclusion that his friend didn't know what he was talking about.

"Me ma's been the man of house longer than me or my da," said Thomas, before turning towards home, happy in the knowledge that at least his father would be present when he got there.

While households throughout the village rang with the sound of families cooking, eating and arguing their way through Sunday dinner, those without the benefit of close relatives took to the drinking establishments for sustenance of a more liquid variety.

Vincent Corrigan and Gerald O'Brien, two of the staunchest proponents of the single life, sat at opposite ends of Hanratty's Bar drinking in silence. Sean Hanratty had left his brother, Peter, to look after the clientele while he partook of the usual

Sunday dinner in his own household.

Vincent looked at the chalkboard above Peter's head displaying five pence ha'penny for a pint. He raised his glass and slurred a toast to no one in particular.

"Here's to the cheapest pint of beer in Cong. My God. Five pence ha'penny a throw. They've fought wars for less."

O'Brien raised his now empty glass to Vincent.

"I hear them film boys are looking for extras down at the fête this afternoon," he told his disinterested drinking companion. "Maybe they'll be doling out the drink for free. What do you say?"

"There's no such thing as free drink," replied Vincent, "not in these parts there isn't. Apart from which I wouldn't work for that Hollywood lot even if they did pay me. It's exploitation, that what it is, is sheer exploitation of the workers. And damn those who let them get away with it."

O'Brien broke into a smile as he found himself in the company of a kindred spirit. He pushed back his chair and made his way over to Vincent's table, ordering two drinks with a thrust of his middle and forefinger in Peter's direction.

O'Brien pulled up a chair opposite Vincent.

"You know it's this electricity stuff I think we should be more worried about, not that film lot," said O'Brien. "The boys from Hollywood, they're going to go away one day but this electricity, I reckon it's going to be around a bit longer than that and it's going to do a damned sight more harm, or my name's not Gerald Michael Collins O'Brien."

"I never knew that."

"Oh it's true right enough. Once the electricity is..."

"No. Not all that electric stuff. I never knew you were named after that traitor Collins."

"What's your middle name? De Valera?"

"You won't draw me into a discussion on the politics of Ireland, past nor present. I was only commenting on your middle name, that's all."

O'Brien's impulse was to wipe the floor with this foolish old man, but he was starting to think that maybe he would have use of Vincent in the days ahead. He ignored the jibe and smiled as best as he could.

"Anyway," continued Vincent, "I don't get your problem."

O'Brien felt the tenuous hold on his temper starting to slip away.

"I don't have a problem with my name," he intoned.

"I'm not talking about your name. I'm back on the electricity now. I don't get your problem. You don't have to have it if you don't want it. That's what I was told."

O'Brien pointed to Vincent, warming to a theme close to his heart.

"Well, that's just where you're wrong, Vincent me boy. Everybody's going to have to have it one day. They're going

122

to put it into your house, it'll end up in the water supply and before you know it the stuff's going to be everywhere, in your food, in your hair, everywhere. And there's nothing you or I can do to stop it."

Peter balanced the two glasses on a small tin tray as he slopped his way across from the bar. O'Brien and Vincent looked on with disdain, neither offering to help the old man as he shuffled towards them. Just as the ancient barman was within a foot or two of the table a loud muffled explosion rent the air causing Peter to jerk in surprise and spill half the beer over the tray and onto the floor.

"What the hell was that?" asked a concerned Vincent.

O'Brien's eyes blazed with self-righteous zeal.

"They're blowing up God's earth to plant the poles that carry the devilish electricity to people who don't want it, that's what they're doing."

As Peter finally managed to rest the overflowing tray on the table O'Brien took one look at the half-empty glasses and laid into him.

"And the rest, old man. Don't think I'm paying you five pence ha'penny for half a - a third of a pint more like. Full measures now. The cheek of it. Five pence ha'penny a pint. It's a disgrace, that's what it is."

"So, you've noticed then?" queried Vincent. "Hanratty's not the only one, either. Landlords," he spat. "They should be hanged, the bloody lot of them."

"Too right," agreed O'Brien. "It's disgusting. The time a decent hard-working man like myself is unable to afford a pint or two any day of the week is the time I'll have to go back to making me own. And that's a pretty desperate state of affairs, I can tell you."

Two full pints finally arrived at the table, much to the delight of a thirsty Vincent and a bleary-eyed O'Brien.

"Hanratty serves a fine pint," Vincent declared. "Even if he is a Protestant heathen.

As both men sipped their beer O'Brien felt heartened by the fact he had finally found the person he had been looking for. Knowing he now had someone with whom the dynamite would be safe for a while, combined with the effects of three pints of beer, was enough to make O'Brien almost genial.

This thin veneer of civility fell away, however, the minute Patrick O'Dea walked into the bar. Patrick nodded to both men as he slid a handful of coins onto the counter.

"A pint of your best please, Peter."

"Look who's here," snapped O'Brien. "Cong's very own prodigal son, Patrick O'Dea, back from the dead and come to grace us with his presence."

"Don't flatter yourself, O'Brien," replied Patrick.

Patrick looked at Vincent.

"Long time no see, you old devil. How you keepin'?"

"Fair, fair," mumbled Vincent.

Patrick turned back to the bar to see Peter staring down at the money.

"What's the problem, never seen real money before?" said Patrick.

"It's not the quality of the coin he's interested in," offered Vincent. "It's the quantity." Peter silently indicated the price on the board. Despite having been back in the village for almost a whole day this was the first time Patrick had actually been moved to provide personal finance – actually Mary's finance if the truth be told - towards the slaking of his thirst and he was visibly shocked. He reached inside his pocket and delved deeply for another coin, finally dropping another penny onto the bar before joining Vincent and O'Brien.

"They'll have to put the price back down as soon as Hollywood goes home, surely?" argued Patrick.

O'Brien snorted, glad to confirm Patrick's worst fears.

"Don't you believe it. I've heard say…" He looked around to ensure nobody else could hear them. "They're going to put the price up even more."

Vincent tapped the edge of the table in exasperation.

"But why, for God's sake?"

"Because somebody's going to have to pay for the electricity, that's why. There's going to be lights all over the place, no privacy for anybody. They're even going to be putting one of them light bulb things in the toilet outside."

This last piece of information evinced a shudder of disgust from both Patrick and Vincent.

"They wouldn't now, would they?" asked Patrick in abhorrence. O'Brien pressed home his case.

"They would. Anything for a profit. And there's that turncoat Gallagher trying to trick the whole village into welcoming the ESB with open arms. Well, he and everybody else can embrace the work of the devil if they want to but count me out. I'll stick with gas and candles if you don't mind."

O'Brien drained his glass with a flourish and wiped the back of his hand across his mouth. It was time to reel Vincent in.

"Vincent, I was wonderin' if you might do me a favour?"

"I knew there was no such thing as a free drink. Not with you there isn't. What do you want?"

O'Brien leaned across the table.

"I need to leave some stuff at your house for a couple of days. Only a couple of day's mind."

"What kind of stuff?" asked Vincent warily. O'Brien touched the side of his nose and slowly lowered the right lid over his bloodshot eye in an attempt to wink secretively.

"The less you know the better," he said, stumbling to his feet. "See you later." O'Brien made for the door leaving Vincent no opportunity to decline his proposal.

Vincent and Patrick sat in silence for a while until Patrick suddenly indicated the barrels of beer behind the bar.

"I could do with one of them to keep me company until Mr Ford and his boys leave and the price stabilises a little, if you get my meaning," said Patrick.

"I'd say it's the least they could give us for putting up with all this inconvenience in our own village," agreed Vincent.

Patrick lowered his voice to a whisper.

"Maybe we'll pay a little visit here one night and liberate a few of them barrels. Just for safe keeping, if you get my drift."

"You're talking rubbish, man," said Vincent. "Besides, Hanratty keeps this place locked tighter than the Bank of Ireland. How on earth would you be able to get in anyway?"

"Oh, don't you worry about that, Vincent me boy," bluffed Patrick. "I'll think of something."

His enigmatic smile hid the fact he had absolutely no idea how to go about breaking into Hanratty's when the time came. Not without getting caught anyway.

Thomas sat at the kitchen table reading one of his cowboy comics while his mother fussed around in the kitchen preparing the midday meal. Thomas could feel the heat from Mary's scowl penetrating the paper as he stared at the comic.

"What are you doing, reading at the meal table like that? Put that rubbish away before I throw it into the dustbin. Your father will be back in a minute. What do you think he'd say?"

He'd say "can I read it when you've finished?" thought Thomas as he obediently put down the comic. Mary called out to Heather with the news that dinner was nearly ready.

Heather appeared a moment later from upstairs wearing her Sunday best plain blue dress.

"Can I help you at all, mother?" asked Heather.

Mary, who had started to spoon out the food, stopped and eyed her children suspiciously.

"I give up. What's going on? What are you two up to?"

Heather and Thomas, now both the picture of angelic innocence, looked at each other and shrugged. Mary pointed at Heather with the wooden spoon she had been to dole out the food, distributing pieces of potato across the table.

"You're up to something." The spoon swivelled in Thomas's direction. "Both of you. You want something. What is it?"

Thomas looked to his sister who then gave him a small nod.

"The fête down at the church, ma. Can we go? Please?"

Mary frowned.

"Since when have either of you ever shown any interest in anything to do with the church?"

Thomas jumped up and down on his chair.

"John Wayne might be there, ma. I want to meet John Wayne. I've seen him but I haven't met him yet."

The front door burst open to reveal Patrick, full of the joy at being reunited once more with his family and the three pints he had put away in Hanratty's.

"What's so special about John Wayne, that's what I'd like to know?" boomed Patrick as he took his place at the head of the table for the second time that day. "Nothing but a jumped-up over-paid Hollywood braggart who couldn't act his way out of a paper bag."

Heather ignored her father and addressed her mother instead.

"Mother, Thomas was telling me that all the stars of the film will be there. And it's for charity. Cruelty to Children." Mary hardly heard a word her daughter said, still too engrossed with the sight of seeing her family together again after two years.

"Patrick, what was that stupid film you took me to see some years back?" asked Mary. "I think he was in that. Terrible he was too."

Patrick shook his head in confusion as Heather decided not to ingratiate herself with her mother any more. It was becoming too demeaning.

"Was he a cowboy?" asked Thomas.

"No," replied Mary. "He certainly wasn't a cowboy, I'd have remembered that. No, he was wearing one of them loincloth things with his chest hanging out for everybody to see. Shameful. Supposed to be a story from the Bible and the man had next to nothing on."

129

Thomas and Heather were totally nonplussed. Patrick had lost the thread by now and wasn't even listening.

"John Wayne?" exclaimed Thomas. His hero would never dress up in such a costume, no matter how much the part called for it.

"That's right!" said Patrick. "He pulled the temple down at the end, smack bang onto his head if I remember rightly."

Mary nodded in full agreement with her husband.

"And good riddance to him, that's what I say," added Patrick, blatantly playing up to his wife. "They should have left him there too."

Thomas felt as though somebody had thumped him in the stomach. Wayne. A sissy. He thought he knew all there was to know about his hero's films but this came as a bitter blow. For a moment Thomas lost all interest in ever wanting to meet Wayne face-to-face. And if such a meeting were to take place where would he look, Thomas thought sadly to himself. Seconds later a trickle of laughter from Heather brought Thomas out of his black mood and back into the light of day.

"Oh, mother," his sister cried, putting her hand to her mouth as she started to giggle. "Samson and Delilah. That's what you're thinking of. And it wasn't John Wayne, it was that other big feller, Victor Whatsisname."

"Mature," said Thomas rather too loudly, glad that Wayne's heroic stature had now been restored in all its rightful glory.

"Exactly," Patrick exclaimed. "They all look the same to me. Which is my point. What's so special about John Wayne, that's what I'd like to know?"

Thomas was just about to answer his father's question with a list of specifics when he was distracted by his mother placing a plate of food in front of him. Without waiting for the rest of the family the young boy practically dive-bombed into the food as Patrick, Mary and Heather dutifully bowed their heads to say grace. Before he could remedy his mistake Thomas was the recipient of yet another clip round the ear, this time from his father.

"Say your prayers, you ungrateful tyke. And let me hear you say it aloud."

Thomas put down the cutlery and clasped his hands tightly together.

"Dear Lord, for what we are about receive, may you make us truly thankful. Amen." As the others added their own Amens, Thomas whispered an addendum to the Lord.

"And please tell people to leave my ears alone. Amen."

"I'm quite sure some of them film folk are nice people, Thomas," Mary went on. "But they're very irreligious. And not one Catholic among them, so I've been told." Both Thomas and Heather looked to the heavens as they prepared themselves for another tirade on the evils of Hollywood. Mary continued.

"Mrs McBride was telling me only the other day that she had to point out to one of them, the man playing one of the priests - Bond I think his name was, little fat feller - she told him that he shouldn't be standing around with his hands in his pockets. No Catholic priest would put his hands in his pocket, she says. Then the man who makes the film, that shifty looking individual with the dark glasses? You know what he says, the blasphemous devil?" asked Mary, pausing dramatically.

The children had heard it at least ten times before, but Patrick was wise enough to show a modicum of interest, lifting his head up from the table to hear the punch-line.

"No, he says," continued Mary. "No Catholic priest would put his hands in his pocket. They only put their hands in other people's pockets. The shame of it. This place will be better for it once they've gone, you can be sure of that."

Patrick nodded and resumed eating.

"What if I went with Tommy, mother?" asked Heather.

Mary looked to her husband to impose his authority. When Patrick just shrugged Heather knew she had won, pressing home her advantage as quickly as possible.

"It's a bit of harmless fun. Come along yourselves, you might enjoy it." Thomas chipped in as he tried to push the discussion towards a satisfactory conclusion.

"Everybody's going, ma, da. Everybody. Please? Can we?" he

asked.

"Charity, you say?" ventured Mary in habitual token resistance to Patrick's obvious acceptance in the matter.

Heather and Thomas nodded.

"And what time does it start?" asked Mary.

"About four o'clock," confirmed Thomas.

"What do you think, Patrick?" Mary asked as she deferred to her husband. Patrick asserted himself.

I want both of you back here in this house no later than five o'clock, you understand me?

His children nodded in grateful unison

"And I'll come looking for the both of you the minute you're late, believe me" promised Mary. They believed her.

The fête attracted people from all over the surrounding area of Cong, filling the small walled enclosure behind the church to capacity. Thomas stood precariously on top of the stone and flint wall on the edge of the grounds trying to get a glimpse of Wayne. He could see Ford, Maureen O'Hara and Victor McLaglen mingling with the crowd and posing for pictures, but Wayne was nowhere to be seen. Thomas knew, however, that the actor would come along sooner or later. Whenever the man in the hat and dark glasses showed up, Wayne was usually never far behind.

Joe watched in bemusement as Gallagher accidentally bumped into Maureen O'Hara, the adoration Gallagher held for the actress on display for everyone to see. Gallagher gulped nervously then ventured a little smile. O'Hara returned the smile even more sweetly, rooting Gallagher to the spot like a statue. With a delicate wave of her hand O'Hara moved on through the crowd. Not just a smile but a wave as well, thought Joe. Gallagher was definitely getting more than he had bargained for there.

Gallagher suddenly burst into life and grabbed Joe by the arm just as Gene and Father Donnelly sauntered past.

"Did you see that then? Did you see?" said Gallagher urgently. "She smiled. At me. She smiled and waved. At me."

"Who smiled at you?" asked Joe disingenuously.

"Miss - Mrs Maureen O'Hara. She smiled straight at me, didn't she? You saw it with your own eyes. Straight at me, she did. She was stood just over there."

He pointed to the spot where the actress had stood before being swallowed up into the crowd. Joe whispered to Gene and pointed behind him.

"Maureen's standing two feet away from me over here. Who's he talking about?"

A moment later Lorna Curtis glided by, sending Gallagher into a frenzy of tie-straightening and masculine preening, as he tugged at the hem of his jacket. Joe looked to both Gene and Father Donnelly, united in their determination not to give the game away as they realised that Gallagher had mistaken Miss Curtis, Maureen O'Hara's stand-in, for the real thing. Joe decided to leave before things turned nasty, making a great show of looking at his watch and studying a clipboard he was carrying before taking his leave.

"Well, I can't stand around here all day. Some of us have to work for a living." He tucked the clipboard under his arm and pushed his way through the gathering, leaving Gene and the Father to cope with the lovelorn Gallagher.

Joe indicated to a group of villagers to line up against the wall of the church. He then walked along taking down the names of the hopeful extras. Thomas, Billy and Michael ran to join the end of the line. Right next to Michael Cassidy. Joe looked up from his clipboard just before he reached the three boys and found himself face to face with the individual who had made him look such a fool the night before.

Cassidy tried his best to stare Joe down but found that without the benefit of large quantities of alcohol his adversary in love could match him glare for glare. Despite his dislike for Cassidy he didn't want what had happened between them to colour his judgement when it came to choosing the extras for the fight scene. After an eternity his good nature won through. "Name?"

Cassidy smiled triumphantly.

"Cassidy. Michael Cassidy."

Joe was about to inform him that they were all to meet next Saturday down at Ashford Farm when he caught Cassidy looking over his shoulder. Joe turned to see Heather standing on the edge of the crowd.

"I'll be through here in a minute," Joe called out to her.

Directing his attention once more to the task at hand Joe caught Cassidy surveying Heather with a look so lascivious it was all he could do to keep himself from smashing Cassidy against the wall and have done with it. He struck Cassidy's name from the clipboard instead.

"Sorry. We've got all the people we need. Try again some other time."

As Joe moved towards Thomas and his friends he felt Cassidy's tight grip on his left shoulder.

"You took my name."

Joe brought himself up to his full height and shook Cassidy's hand away.

"I was curious. Just wanted to know in case we met again."

"Don't you have any fear on that score, Yank. We'll most definitely be meeting again. I'll make sure of it."

Joe and Heather watched Cassidy as he stomped away through the crowd. Joe then turned and knelt down to talk to Thomas and his friends.

"I'm sorry, boys, but we're not looking for any kids in this scene. Just people who are, well… older. Maybe another time, okay?"

As the dejected boys walked away Joe took a couple of wrappers of gum from his pocket and handed them to Thomas in consolation. Thomas smiled then ran off with his friends. Joe shook his head and appealed to Heather.

"If I could I'd have hired them. Honest."

"I know. It's just that he's set his heart so on meeting John Wayne before the film finishes."

Joe leaned closer and whispered to her.

"Come for a walk and I'll see what I can do."

Heather affected a look of mild shock then playfully fluttered her eyelids.

"Why, Mr Yates, what kind of person do you take me for?"

"Come for a walk and I'll tell you," pleaded Joe.

Heather pointed to the other end of the church wall.

"Go round to the front of the church. I'll see you in a minute. We don't want the whole village knowing we're walking out with each other now, do we?"

Nobody noticed either of them as Joe and Heather appeared to walk away in different directions. Nobody that is except Patrick O'Dea who had managed to slip out of the house and now stood with his son watching with mounting interest from the crowd as his daughter conversed with one of the Yanks. Patrick pointed to Joe as he disappeared around the corner of the church.

"That feller over there. What was he saying to you and Heather?"

Thomas knew better than to conceal the truth from his father. So he decided to tell half the story now and the rest, the part concerning his sister, at a later and more convenient date.

"He was looking for people to be in a fight scene with John Wayne. Told us we were too young."

Patrick put his arm around his son and pulled him close.

"Too young? Well, let's see what your father can do about that. I've never let you down yet, have I?"

Despite his age Thomas knew when to be truthful and when to be diplomatic.

"Never, da. Never."

"That's my boy. Now you run along and stay out of trouble. I'm going to see a man about a job."

Joe and Heather leaned against the front wall of the church, holding hands in the bright sunlight.

"We're shooting at the church tomorrow. Why don't you come down, take a look and see what I do for a living?"

She squeezed his hand.

"Okay. What time?"

Joe shrugged.

"Any time. We'll probably be there most of the day depending on how the weather holds."

Heather pulled Joe towards her.

"That's a good thing, then, isn't it?" she said, smiling.

"Why is that?" asked Joe, not in the faintest bit interested in what Heather was saying to him as they turned to embrace each other.

"You can spend more time in the evening with me."

Joe closed his eyes as his lips lightly brushed her perfumed cheek. He put both arms around her waist and was just about to kiss her when his concentration was broken by the sound of a polite cough.

"Nice day for it, don't you think?" said Patrick.

Joe and Heather quickly released each other.

"We were..."

"I saw," said Patrick, interrupting his daughter. "Where's your manners, young lady? Aren't you going to introduce us?"

Heather stepped away from Joe, angry at being caught out by her father.

"Joe, this is my father, Patrick. Patrick O'Dea."

Joe nodded nervously at Heather's father.

"Father, this is Joseph Yates. He's from America."

Patrick advanced towards Joe, his hand outstretched in welcome.

"Pleased to make your acquaintance, Mr Yates."

As they shook hands Patrick looked at Joe while addressing his daughter.

"Heather, be a good girl there now and go see that little brother of yours. Make sure he's not up to no good. You know how his mother frets. Me and Joseph here, we've got a little business to discuss."

Joe tensed his muscles against Patrick's interminable handshake.

"I've been away."

"So I gathered," answered Joe, giving Heather a what-the-hell-is-going-on-here? look. She shrugged and walked off, leaving the two men to converse in private. Joe took a deep breath in readiness for the verbal – at least he was hoping it was going to be just verbal – assault from Heather's father.

Thomas found himself separated from Billy and Michael as he wandered through the crowd in search of Wayne. Looking behind him for a moment Thomas stumbled into a space in the crowd and bounced off a large pair of legs planted firmly in the ground. He fell onto his back, cursing at the great lummox in front of him as he propped himself up onto his elbows.

"Hey, you big eejit, look where you're going."

The big man turned around to see who had knocked in to him. Thomas looked up and found himself staring straight at the sun, dazzling his sight for a moment and obscuring the face of the man towering above him. Half-blinded by the brightness Thomas did not realise who he had bumped into, but the voice was instantly recognisable as the man lifted him easily from the ground.

"Kind of in a hurry, ain't you kid?" said John Wayne, rendering Thomas speechless. As he got over the shock of finally meeting the actor up close, Michael and Billy materialised out of nowhere, their jaws dropping in admiration at the sight of Wayne talking to their friend. The actor reached into his pocket and drew out three Irish shillings.

"Say, do me a favour. I seem to have run out of cigarettes. See if you can fetch me some. Is that shop over there open?"

Wayne pointed to McGowran's grocery shop next to the post office on the other side of the road. Thomas nodded as Wayne handed him the money, backing away quickly in his eagerness to please.

"Don't take too long now," Wayne gently chided him. "I'll be waiting right here for you." Without saying a word Thomas turned and ran across the road towards McGowran's, his two friends in hot pursuit.

"Did you see that?" said Thomas, unable to conceal his excitement. "Did you hear? He talked to me. John Wayne talked to me!"

"Lucky you didn't bump into him too hard," said Michael. "Next time he might shoot you."

"Not if I see him first he won't."

Thomas drew his 'gun' and pointed at Michael and Billy, the boys returning their fire as they all ran towards the door of the shop.

A wizened old man in his eighties, McGowran had opened the shop on a Sunday to take advantage of the potential customers across the road attending the fête. Business had been slow just the same and McGowran was just about to close and join the money-pinching ingrates at the church when the door burst open to reveal a breathless Thomas, Billy and Michael keeping their distance as they peeked around the door into the shop.

"What do you want?" snapped McGowran as he started to lock the till. Thomas approached the counter holding out the money at arm's length.

"I want some cigarettes please," said Thomas. McGowran greeted this ridiculous request with a look of alarm.

"You trying to get me put away or something?" he said, pointing accusingly with an unsteady hand at the boy.

"They're not for me," wailed Thomas. "They're for John Wayne. He sent me over especially with the money. Look." As he held the coins under McGowran's nose the shop keeper grabbed Thomas by the ear. Not the left ear. Not the one that nobody ever tweaked, pulled, twisted or maligned in ways too numerous and cruel to mention but the right ear. The one ear all residents in Cong appeared to gravitate towards whenever they wished to register disapproval of Thomas O'Dea by attempting to separate the appendage from the side of his head. McGowran was obviously no exception to this cruel ritual as he pinched and twisted Thomas' sore flesh.

"I know who you are, Thomas O'Dea," McGowran started to shout as he began to shuffle round the counter. "And I'll be talking to your mother first chance I get. Now. Out. The lot of you. John Wayne, you say. Whatever next." The old man shooed a disappointed Thomas and the other boys from the shop, slamming the door shut behind them.

"The nerve of it. John Wayne," spat McGowran as he made his way towards the back of the shop. "Now. If the smokes were for Barry Fitzgerald then it might have been a different story."

As the boys slouched around outside the shop wondering what to do next Vincent Corrigan walked slowly up the road towards Hanratty's. In sheer desperation Thomas approached him in the hope that despite his similarity in age to McGowran, Corrigan could not possibly be more miserable than the old shop keeper, illustrating Thomas's failings when it came to judgement of character. Michael and Billy had no such illusions regarding Corrigan, keeping well out of the way as Thomas stood in front of Vincent.

"Mr Corrigan, sir, I was just wondering if you might be doing me a favour, if you'd be so kind?"

Vincent stared impatiently at the boy.

"If it's money you're after, steal it from somebody else, you little beggar."

Vincent started to push Thomas out of the way.

"No, Mr Corrigan, I don't want money. I have it, see. I just want you to..."

Vincent saw the coins in the boy's hand and stopped.

"What do you want?" he snarled. Thomas took a deep breath as the story gushed forth in a deluge of unpunctuated syntax.

"You see John Wayne's given me three shillings to buy some cigarettes for him, and Mr McGowran in the shop there thinks that the cigarettes are actually for me but they're not for me they're for John Wayne who gave me the money to buy them in the first place and he's over there by the church waiting for me to bring him the cigarettes and if I don't there'll be hell to pay so I was wonderin' if you might nip into the shop and buy the cigarettes for me so's I can give them to John Wayne like I promised."

Thomas ducked as the standard reaction towards him set in, Vincent's hand missing the side of the boy's head by a whisker before setting off towards Hanratty's, muttering curses beneath his breath.

"I can't wait 'til I grow up and people stop hitting me around the ear," lamented Thomas.

"I can't wait to see what happens when John Wayne finds out you haven't got his smokes for him," laughed Billy. "A clipped ear will be the least of your troubles, I'll bet."

Thomas made his mournful way back towards the fête, his friends giggling behind him.

Gene, Bo and Father Donnelly watched from a distance as Gallagher posed for a photograph with 'Maureen O'Hara', Gallagher struggling to hold his stomach in as the photographer focused on the pair of them.

Gene shook his head.

"Father, this is cruel. Somebody's going to have to break it to him. He's walked past the real Maureen O'Hara about five times already while spending the last half hour mooning over her stand-in. We should tell him. It would be the Christian thing to do."

Donnelly nodded.

"True, it would be the Christian thing to do, Mr Willis, but would it be the Catholic thing to do, I ask myself?"

Gallagher stood stock still with a beaming smile pasted on his face as the photographer clicked the shutter. He then turned towards Lorna Curtis and daintily kissed her hand.

"Such a delight to meet a real gentleman, I'm sure," said Lorna, the soft Irish lilt in her voice warming Gallagher's thumping heart. He produced a small notebook and pen from his jacket pocket for her to autograph.

"I wonder if it wouldn't be too much of a bother for a fine lady such as yourself to maybe sign your autograph," asked Gallagher, his face flushed with excitement. "For my sister, of course."

"Of course."

Lorna, smiling as she started to sign her name, looked up at Gallagher who was still grinning like an idiot.

"It's for you really, isn't it?"

"Er - well - yes, to be exact, if I'm truthful, Miss... er... never had a sister actually, and no brothers either, come to that, just me and me mother, but she's not here today, she's feeling a touch poorly. It's just me. On me own."

Gene was unable to watch anymore, burying his head in his hands as Gallagher started to crumble. Father Donnelly smiled benignly as he witnessed first hand the weakness of the flesh when confronted by beauty. Bo went looking for Wayne, hoping to entice him into the nearest pub.

"What's your name?" asked Lorna as Gallagher's speech dried up.

"Gallagher. Dermot Joseph Edward Aloycius Gallagher."

Lorna wrote her name and his onto the notebook with a

flourish then handed the book and pen back.

"There you are, Dermot. A pleasure to have met you." As Lorna walked away she turned and gave Gallagher a tiny wave of her hand. He bowed extravagantly in return, clutching the precious notebook to his chest as he rejoined Gene and Donnelly.

"That Maureen. I think she's sweet on me. What do you think, Gene? Reckon I stand a chance? She might be married but you know what these Hollywood marriages are like," babbled a love-stricken Gallagher. "One minute they're traipsing down the aisle then before the honeymoon's over they're off to Rio or Reno or wherever the place is for a quickie divorce and..." he clicked his fingers, "...wheel on the next husband."

Gene swallowed as he tried communicating telepathically with Father Donnelly in an effort to make him put the poor man out of his misery.

"Well," said Gene, pointing to the notebook, "at least you've got her autograph. Something to show the grandchildren, anyhow."

Gallagher held out the notebook in front of him and proudly read the inscription.

To my friend Dermot Joseph Edward Aloycius Gallagher. Best Wishes - Lorna Curtis.

Gallagher's smile faltered as he squinted at the writing, pulling the book closer to his face.

"Lorna Curtis? Who the hell....?"

Gallagher stopped and looked over his shoulder towards Lorna.

"Is that her real name? Lorna Curtis? I thought it was Maureen O'Hara."

Gallagher's look of concern changed to one of enlightenment as the explanation dawned upon him.

"She must have changed it, you see, make it sound a bit more Hollywood-like, I suppose, isn't that right, Gene?"

Gene shook his head.

"No, Dermot, that woman you just spoke to really is Lorna Curtis. She's Maureen O'Hara's stand-in. That's the real Maureen O'Hara. Over there."

He pointed towards the actress standing next to Wayne and Ford a few yards away. Gallagher blinked once more at the notebook in confusion.

"But..." He looked towards Lorna Curtis. "She looks more like Maureen O'Hara than Maureen O'Hara does herself. It can't be."

"I'm afraid that's Hollywood for you, Dermot. When it comes to the silver screen, the camera always lies."

Gallagher dredged up a crooked smile.

"Made a bit of a fool of myself now, didn't I?"

Gene and the priest shook their heads and uttered denials far too quickly for Gallagher to believe in the credibility of their assurances.

"Nothing of the sort, Dermot," lied Gene. "Now. Would you like to meet the real Miss O'Hara? I could arrange an introduction for you right this minute."

Gallagher found himself turning down an opportunity he never thought in his wildest dreams would ever have come his way.

"Thanks, Gene, but I think maybe I'll give it a miss if you don't mind. Maybe some other time. Make my apologies to Miss O'Hara, if you'd be so kind."

Gene put a friendly hand on Gallagher's shoulder.

"See you over at Ryan's later on. Okay?"

Gallagher nodded miserably then walked away, dropping the notebook as he made his way out of the church grounds.

Patrick indicated a small path leading out of the front of the church towards the bridge where Heather had taken Joe the night before.

"Let's go for a walk."

Joe demurred, reluctant to 'discuss business' with her wayward father in such an intimate place. He in turn indicated a pathway next to the river that lead towards Ashford Castle then walked off without giving Patrick the option to argue about it either way.

A young couple walked hand-in-hand a few yards in front of them as if to aggravate Joe at the thought of spending such a beautiful day in the company of the wrong member of the family O'Dea. It was a few moments before he broke the silence, frustrated at having to stop every few feet and wait for Patrick to catch up to him, his lanky legs carrying Joe twice as far as Heather's father with each step.

"Okay. What do you want?" Joe asked sullenly.

Patrick stopped and picked a long blade of grass from the overgrown river bank. As he faced the river and chewed on the grass in contemplation Joe sat on the edge of the river and dangled his feet just above the water.

"Do you love her?" asked Patrick suddenly.

Joe smiled at the memory of the night before.

"Well, we've really only just met, but if there's such a thing as love at first sight, then I truly love your daughter, Mr O'Dea."

"Are you going to make a good woman of her?"

"Of course I am. What kind of person do you take me for?"

Patrick sat down beside him.

"And are you going to provide for her, look after her, do all the things a good husband should do for the woman he loves? Are you going to do all those things for my Heather, Mr Yates?"

Joe didn't even have to think about it.

"I'll do all those things and more. You have my word."

"That's good to hear. And now you know what I want."

Joe fell silent for a moment, still not sure of what it was Patrick really did want.

"You want me to look after Heather?" said a tentative Joe.

"Yes. I want you to look after my Heather. Just as I want to be able to look after my wife. I want to give Mary all the things I could never give her before. That's what I want, to be a provider. A man can't ask for more than that now, can he?"

Joe caught on to Patrick's meaning.

"And I suppose I'm in a position to help you in that respect, is that right, Mr O'Dea?"

Patrick got to his feet and slapped Joe on the shoulder.

"Got it in one, Mr Yates. By the way, the name's Patrick. Pleased to meet you." He spat on his hand and proffered it to Joe as the young man got up from the ground. Anything for a peaceful life, thought Joe, as he extended his hand.

"The boys, too." added Patrick, "I'm sure they'd love to be in the film as well."

Joe dithered, not liking the way in which he was being coerced into taking on more extras than he needed. And child extras at that, for a scene in which no children were required. He'd probably get Hell from the old man for this but Patrick was Heather's father after all and besides, it was better to have Patrick on his side rather than against him. They shook hands,

Joe hoping he would not come to regret Patrick's powers of persuasion.

Thomas never thought that he would find himself not wanting to talk to John Wayne, but his failure to fetch the actor his cigarettes took all the joy out of having finally met his hero in the first place. Wayne had his back to the boy, conversing with Ford and McLaglen. Thomas stood behind the big man and tugged lightly on Wayne's jacket.

"I'm sorry," gulped Thomas, near to tears. "But they wouldn't let me buy the cigarettes for you. I'm too young." He held out his hand to give the money back to Wayne.

The big actor knelt down, a big smile breaking across his face which immediately put Thomas' mind at rest.

"Don't you worry about it, kid. Thanks for trying. Keep the money." Wayne stood as a grateful Thomas ran off to join his friends.

"Hey Pappy," said Wayne to Ford. "Give me one of those cheroots you keep chewin' on."

Thomas clutched the three shiny coins Wayne had bequeathed him, vowing that he would never spend them as long as he lived. Michael and Billy tried to be happy for their friend but in truth were somewhat disappointed that Wayne hadn't killed Thomas with his bare hands right in front of their eyes.

"You should ask John Wayne if you can be in his film. Seeing as he's a pal of yours now," suggested Billy.

Thomas heard the slight envy in Billy's voice but chose not to rise to the occasion. A moment later Patrick popped out of the crowd and bore down on the group of boys with a wide grin on his face.

"We're in, Thomas me boy, we're in, all of us," announced a proud Patrick to the bemused looking boys. "Your da has put the fix in for us to be in the film with the Big Fella over there."

As Patrick pointed towards Wayne, Thomas knew instinctively that now was not the time to tell of his momentous encounter with the Big Fella himself. After all, there was only room for one self-satisfied individual at that moment. Thomas graciously gave his father the floor as he and his friends reacted to the news.

"We're in the film? Is that really true, da, we're really going to be in a film with John Wayne?" Patrick presided gratifyingly over a cacophony of cheers and loud exaltations as the boys jumped up and down excitedly.

"You see?" grinned Patrick to his son. "I told you to leave it to the old man."

"How did you do it?" asked Billy.

"Pulled a few strings, spoke to the right people,"

"How much are they paying us?" asked Michael.

"Ah - it's gettin' late, boys," said a flustered Patrick. "Me and Tommy here, we'd best be getting back before mother starts wondering where we are. Tea's early today."

Patrick steered his son in front of him as Thomas waved goodbye to his friends.

Joe returned to the front of the church to find Heather standing just inside the open doorway.

"Why did you run off?"

"What did he want?" said a tight-lipped Heather.

"Just some work. Said he needed the money because he wanted to provide for his family."

"He needs the money alright. But not so he can provide for us. He just wants to get a skinful whenever he feels like it."

Heather's contempt for her father put Joe on the defensive.

"Hey, don't put the blame on me now. He asked me if I could get him a job on the film and..."

"And what?" snapped Heather. "What did he offer to do for you in return?"

Joe scratched his head as he thought about this for a moment.

"Well, I guess... I guess he didn't really offer me anything at all, he just kind of implied..."

"Implied what?"

Joe shrugged.

"He – you know - that things - you and me - he wouldn't stand in the way. I guess. I dunno. He…"

Joe ran out of words. Heather stood silently in the shadows,

154

habit causing her to try and figure out what her father might be up to. Joe held out his arms as he tried to reason with her.

"Hey, he's your father. I mean, aren't you glad he's back?"

"My mother and Thomas are happy he's back. As for me, I couldn't care one way or the other."

She walked away so quickly it took a few seconds before Joe realised Heather wasn't there anymore. At that moment Gene turned the corner of the church on his way back to Ashford Castle.

"She just took off," said Joe to his friend. "One minute she was standing right here, the next - gone.". Joe sighed in frustration and scratched his head. "I just don't understand this whole man and woman thing."

"You wouldn't be the first, kiddo, that's for sure," said Gene. "You wouldn't be the first."

CHAPTER FIVE

The following day Joe and the rest of the crew gathered outside the Church of Ireland in Cong and began to position the lights and camera in front of the main entrance. The scene to be shot involved the first meeting of Sean Thornton and Mary Kate Danaher, as played by Wayne and Maureen O'Hara. Their hands touch as they wash in the font placed outside the church. Barry Fitzgerald, playing the part of the local village matchmaker, accuses the couple of playing 'patty fingers' without having been introduced to each other first. Thus the stormy romance begins between Thornton and Danaher.

The diminutive Barry Fitzgerald sat on top of a horse-drawn carriage rehearsing his lines while the stand-ins for Wayne and O'Hara helped Ford to line up the shot. Joe stood to one side watching as the crew went about their business. Ford sat in his canvas chair next to the camera, and lit his pipe as he called out instructions to the cast and crew. His eyes were hidden as usual behind dark glasses, but everybody was so tuned in to Ford's wayward temperament that it soon became clear something was not quite right. Work slowly came to a halt, all eyes turning towards Ford who held a burning match above his unlit pipe.

"Where's the font?" growled the director. "We can't shoot the goddam scene without the goddam font."

Ford snapped at Gene Willis who stood nearby.

"You. Call yourself a props man? Find me a goddam font. Now."

Gene and Bo hurried out of the church to hunt down the missing prop. Knowing that Ford had eyes in the back of his head Joe faded from view and made his way over to the side of the church where he could not be seen. As he crept along the wall he saw Heather peeping around the corner of the church to look for him. He moved towards her as she withdrew, then caught her by surprise as she looked back around the corner once more.

"Oh, you gave me such a fright!" she gasped. "What are you doing here?"

Joe laughed quietly so as not attract Ford's attention.

"We're shooting the patty fingers scene. That man over there..." Joe pointed out Barry Fitzgerald, "...is kind of like the village matchmaker so he's gonna bawl out Wayne for

trying to get too familiar with O'Hara her outside the church."

"But this is a Protestant church," said a puzzled Heather. "When you said come down to the church today I assumed you meant where they held the fête yesterday. The Catholic church. My church."

"What's the difference? A church is a church, isn't it?"

Although Joe could see Heather was genuinely shocked at his

ignorance, he remained steadfastly nonplussed.

Ford's voice suddenly rung out loud and clear across the church yard, homing in on Joe like radar and moving Heather to jump back around the corner.

"When you've finished playing 'patty fingers' with the ladies of the village, Mr Yates, maybe you'll find some time to help me shoot this picture. If that's not too inconvenient of course." Ford's voice raised a register. "And where's that goddammed font?"

"Stay here," Joe ordered Heather. "I'll be back in a minute."

Joe rushed back to the set just in time to catch Gene and Bo struggling through the gates with a large stone font. Ford clapped his hands in delight.

"Perfect. That looks great."

Ford got up from his chair and wandered over to the church entrance.

"Put it right here. Looks good. Where'd the hell you get it from?"

Gene pointed breathlessly over his shoulder.

"We asked this real nice guy just outside the gates here if he knew where we might find one of these things. We paid him five pounds and he took us back to that church we were at yesterday and damned if there wasn't one there all the time."

"The people here, they're so friendly," enthused a sweating Bo. "And this country. Nothing but a mass of churches and pubs."

"Drinking and praying are the two national pastimes of the Irish," offered Ford. "I thank Christ for the first one and as for the second, I can only give thanks to the Almighty that I was born in America. Okay. Rehearsal!"

Patrick examined the large five-pound note given to him by those wonderful film boys, holding it up to the light to make sure he hadn't been passed a counterfeit. Convinced that it was the genuine article he folded it carefully and placed it in the top pocket of his threadbare jacket, whistling to himself at the thought of having done a good day's work long before the sun had finished climbing in the sky. It was also a fine state of affairs when the only matter to concern him was which drinking establishment he should grace first with his presence on such a lovely summers day, Ryan's or Hanratty's.

With Ford engrossed in setting up the shot in front of the church, Joe slid off once more to join Heather. He found her leaning against the wall with her arms folded, watching the small figure of her father hopping jauntily down the road.

Having witnessed the financial transaction that had taken place between Patrick and Gene a few moments before, she found herself torn between telling Joe what she knew of the arrangement or just letting matters take their natural course.

The truth would come out sooner or later, Heather convinced herself, by which time she hoped to have made a clean break from Cong and the ties that bound her to the village.

"I guess I've got a lot to learn about Ireland still, huh?" admitted Joe.

"It would certainly help to distinguish between a Catholic and a Protestant church for a start," she chided him. "And a font, come to that," she added inadvertently, a slip of the tongue that she instantly regretted.

"Font?" Heather took Joe's hand and pulled him around the corner of the church. Taking a deep breath, she pointed towards the font in the doorway.

"You've just placed a holy Catholic font in front of a Protestant church. There'll be hell to pay."

"But it's only a font."

"Don't say I didn't warn you. You'll be starting a holy war in this village before you're through. Mind you, this place could do with a little scandal every now and then. It's not the most exciting place to live in, I can tell you."

Joe found himself appreciating for the first time how important it was for Heather to get away from the village before it crushed the spirit from her. He fought a ridiculous romantic urge to sweep her up in his arms and run with her into the hills and mountains of Connemara, where they could live unhindered and untouched by the pettiness of life. He momentarily lost the fight and moved forward to hold her. Reality interrupted once more in the guise of a bellowing Ford.

"Mr Yates. If you please."

Joe faltered as Ford's voice drained the urgency and momentum from his body. Heather stood on her toes and kissed him on the cheek.

"Your master calls, and so does mine. I have to get back to the shop."

"Can I walk you home?" asked Joe.

"Five o'clock. And only to the corner, mind."

A loud incoherent shout of rage from Ford broke the hold they had on each other. Heather slipped away behind the church and Joe hurried back to the set

Vincent Corrigan's cottage lay on the edge of Cong next to the road leading out of the village towards Claremorris. The 'cottage' was in reality little more than a number of rooms thrown together over a period of time to form a large pile of stones in which Vincent sheltered from the wind and rain. He had lived there by himself for the best part of thirty years since the passing of his mother and father. They had both drowned together in nearby Lough Corrib one dark moonless night when their coracle sprung a leak while out stealing fish from a fisherman's net.

Apart from the cottage itself Vincent inherited all of his parents' earthly goods consisting of a wooden table, a tin bath, four rickety chairs, a three legged bed and an ancient wood-fired stove. The table and chairs were consigned to the stove one particularly harsh winter's night, while the bath was used primarily to catch the water dripping through a large hole in the roof at the back of the house.

Due to Vincent's aversion to the female of the species, the bed had never been called upon to undergo anything more strenuous than the tossing and turning of a heavily inebriated Vincent wrestling with a bottle of home-made poteen. The three-legged piece of furniture therefore still proved fairly robust, springs included. As for the mattress, the least described the better.

Later that afternoon Vincent busied himself in the small back room of his home, tinkering with a small valve located above the drip tap on his illicit still. The design of the still had been about as well planned as Vincent's house, with cracked copper piping and sections of thin glass tubing meandering along the back wall from floor to ceiling like a bundle of glass and steel entrails.

He carefully adjusted the spitting flame hurtling from a rusty Bunsen burner that should have been consigned to the rubbish dump at least ten years before the outbreak of the

Great War. As Vincent adjusted the heat from the burner, a loud thump on the front door broke his concentration, causing him to burn his fingers on the hot metal. Cursing loudly with practised vehemence, Vincent frantically hid various stirring utensils and bags of sugar and oats like some demented scientist from a horror movie desperate to conceal the cadavers before the villagers break down the door and burn him and the laboratory to the ground. The incessant knocking combined with Vincent's burnt fingertips and imminent heart failure roused him to anger.

"Jesus, Mary and Joseph! Stop that infernal racket, you'll knock me bloody door in!"

Kicking the last sack of sugar into the bottom of a small cupboard, Vincent threw aside the tattered curtain that hung in the doorway between the back room and the living area and moved towards the front door, sucking on his fingers to ease the pain. Not knowing who to expect, Vincent threw open the large wooden door to find himself confronting none other than his erstwhile drinking companion, Gerald O'Brien. The unexpected visitor stood in the doorway, his collar pulled up around his neck as he glanced furtively behind him, ignorant of the mayhem he had just unleashed within.

"For God's sake, man, why the hell didn't you speak up? I thought it might be the Garda come for me still, you brainless goon!" yelled Vincent.

As O'Brien pushed his way into the house, Vincent could see he was trying to conceal something beneath his jacket. O'Brien sniffed the air in disgust.

"My God, Corrigan, this place stinks like a brewery. It's a wonder the whole bloody village can't smell it down there."

"Mind your own damned business," replied Vincent as he slammed the door and willed his heartbeat back to some sense of normality. "What do you want?"

O'Brien put his finger to his mouth then revealed the two bundles of dynamite he had hidden inside his jacket.

"What the hell are you doing, bringing that stuff into my house?" shrieked Vincent, finding it hard to believe that even somebody as stupid as O'Brien could walk around with a handful of explosives secreted under his coat.

O'Brien's eyes took on a strange faraway look as he held the sticks of dynamite in front of him.

"It's the stuff those devils from the ESB have been using to blast away half of the mountains in and around Cong in order to plant the poles. I have snatched them from the hands of the filthy capitalist swine who have dared to desecrate and rape our valley with their infernal electricity."

Any other person finding themselves in the company of Gerald O'Brien at that precise moment would have been looking to make their excuses and leave. Vincent, however, was still too angry at this unwanted intrusion to feel anything other than contempt towards his intruder.

"You're stark raving mad. Besides which, Cong is not situated in a valley and as for the mountains, they're miles away. How long have you actually lived here?"

O'Brien shook a fistful of explosives in Vincent's direction. Vincent instinctively backed away to the other side of the room.

"Gallagher and those other lackeys of the ESB are planning a celebration when they switch on the power in the village. I've decided to have a little party of me own. They put up the poles. I'm going to take them down. Boom."

Vincent jumped in agitation as O'Brien traced a giant explosion in the air with his hands.

"Once the poles are down and their precious schedule has gone up in smoke, they'll be forced to put the wires across my land and I'll finally get what is rightfully mine."

Vincent was appalled.

"You're mad. You hear me? Crazy. You'll never get away with it. Never."

O'Brien's eyes narrowed.

"Nobody need ever know. Unless you tell them, of course."

Vincent was too proud to let such a slur go unremarked.

"How dare you, O'Brien, I'm no informer. I'm no freedom fighter either, and you have no business bringing dynamite into my house."

O'Brien dropped his voice to a loud whisper.

"I need you to take care of it for me. They might find it at my place."

"And who are they?" asked a disturbed Vincent, tuning in to O'Brien's state of mind.

"Never you mind. Just keep it safe here for a few days and then it'll be off your hands before you know it."

"Why should I put my neck out for you?"

O'Brien winked.

"Because once the ESB see things my way I'll compensate you for your trouble."

Vincent weighed up his options, deciding it was better and a damned sight safer to go along with O'Brien for the moment, then get rid of the explosives at a later date.

"If it's still here by next Friday I'll be wanting quite a lot of compensation, I can tell you that."

O'Brien just shrugged and handed over the dynamite.

"Please yourself," he said, before looking around the sparsely furnished room.

"Got anything to drink then?"

The loud whistling of boiling liquid suddenly screamed from behind the curtained door, signalling the imminent production of a new batch of poteen. Vincent hurried off to turn down the heat on the still then returned moments later with two bottles of recent vintage, having decided not to waste any of the new stuff on O'Brien. He held the bottles up for inspection.

"Sweet or dry?"

O'Brien looked from one bottle to the other and pondered for a moment.

"Hmmm," he finally ventured. "I could chance me arm with the dishwater from the bottle on the left, or go for the yellow mouse piss in the other. However, judging by the state of your face I'd have to say I don't care which one I have, as long as it's not the one you've been drinking."

"Ah," replied Vincent. "In that case then, you'll be wanting the dry."

CHAPTER SIX

The following morning Mary O'Dea was busying herself clearing up after breakfast. Thomas had left a few moments before telling his mother he and his friends would be down by Ashford Castle where they intended to replicate Custer's Last Stand with two Indians, Custer, a toy gun and a couple of home-made bows and arrows. "And if the little tyke gets an arrow in his eye," she suddenly thought, "he'd better not come crying to me". After Heather left for work Patrick assured his loving wife he would be spending his time in pursuit of a fair day's work for a fair day's pay and had left with hearty promises of resuming his place as the breadwinner of the family. As the golden rays of the sun shone through the kitchen window illuminating her humble surroundings in God-given light, Mary was hard put to remember the last time she had felt such contentment.

Then came Father Donnelly.

Mary answered the knock on the door with a tea cloth in her hand and happiness in her heart, her near-religious exaltation abruptly terminated when she saw the father standing in front of her. The priest was smiling, but a slight hardness around the eyes gave him away. This was not a social visit.

"Good day to you, Mrs O'Dea. A wonderful morning, don't you think?" he said, displaying a priest's innate talent for small talk. It had been, thought Mary, but not any longer. She bobbed stiffly and opened the door wider.

"Please, father. Come in. I was just clearing up. Excuse the mess, if you don't mind."

She offered him a chair then hurried to clear away the rest of the breakfast dishes before rejoining him at the table.

"Would you like some tea?" asked Mary.

"No thank you, Mrs O'Dea," Donnelly replied with a smile.

"Most definitely not a social visit," Mary thought to herself.

They sat opposite each other in silence for a few moments, neither wanting to initiate what was obviously going to be a painful conversation. Mary proved braver than Donnelly, pitching in to get it over and done with.

"So, Father. What can I be doing for you? It's not very often you visit so you must have something on your mind."

"I do, Mrs O'Dea, something of a personal nature, I'm afraid."

"It's Heather, isn't it?" said Mary in a rush. "I knew it. That blasted girl, what's she done now, father? Tell me and I'll have it out with her the minute she gets home, you see if I don't. She's eighteen going on thirty-five and she thinks the world revolves around her. Just you wait until I see her, I'll..."

Mary stopped as Father Donnelly shook his head and raised his hand to stop her in mid-diatribe.

"Your daughter is a paragon of virtue compared to some of the other young ladies hereabouts, Mrs O'Dea. You should be proud of her. Heather is not the reason I'm here, I can assure you."

Mary sighed inwardly with relief.

"Then it must be Thomas," she said, denying the obvious reason for the priest's visit but knowing deep down that he could only be sitting in front of her for one reason and one person only. Father Donnelly shook his head once more.

"It's not Thomas either, Mrs O'Dea."

Mary clasped her hands to her chest, choosing to stare at the table rather than look the priest in the face.

"What's he done, father?"

Donnelly took a deep breath and placed his elbows on the table, his hands clasped gravely beneath his chin.

"Your husband sold the holy font from our church to Mr Ford's film crew for five pounds."

Her hand flew to her mouth in shock.

"I'll kill the little..." Mary stopped and recovered herself, her face turning a ruddy pink.

"I'm sorry, Father. Please forgive me." Donnelly shrugged and smiled wryly.

"Totally understandable, Mrs O'Dea. I think I'd have to renounce the cloth before I could ever be compelled to tell you what went through my mind when I found out, that's for sure."

Mary was stunned at Patrick's behaviour, whispering Hail Mary's to herself over and over again as she begged an unforgiving God for absolution in exchange for her soul. Father Donnelly paused diplomatically before delivering the final blow. Mary stopped praying as he cleared his throat.

"There's something else?" asked Mary, wide-eyed in horror. This time it was Donnelly's turn to look away.

"They took our holy Catholic font and put it outside the Church of Ireland. Reverend Casey turned it into a bird bath."

Just before Mary passed out the thought occurred to her that the Vatican would most certainly revise its intransigent position regarding divorce were Patrick O'Dea to land on their doorstep. And God help him when he landed on hers.

Thomas had made it plain to his friends that although it was a well known fact General Custer had indeed perished with all his men at the Little Big Horn, he, as Custer, would not be dying as a matter of principle. Cowboys killed Indians and that's all there was to it. Michael suggested that in that case they should play a game in which the cowboy didn't die, such as Davy Crockett, the famous Indian fighter. Michael volunteered to be Crockett and kill Thomas and Billy who would obviously be the Indians.

Thomas informed Michael that in fact Davy Crockett had died at a place called the Alamo therefore he and Billy should be Mexicans and gut Michael with their wooden bayonets. As Custer and Crockett squared up to each other for a fight, Billy informed both his friends that it was about time they came up with a game that didn't require him to writhe around in agony full of bullets or anything else they could devise to shoot or point in his direction.

He therefore insisted they play Robin Hood instead which was no good to anybody because no one ever wanted to be the Sheriff of Nottingham. At which point Thomas conceded that they could indeed kill Custer, but only for one game. After that they would revert to his preferred version of the truth in which Custer won the day.

The boys retired to the middle of the village in the hot afternoon, having exhausted themselves re-enacting the bloodiest Wild West scenarios they could come up with - from the gunfight at the O.K. Corral to the death of Billy the Kid. The latter provided Billy, by dint of his name, the only opportunity to actually get to play a cowboy. Albeit one with a brief lifespan.

They watched the crew set up another shot by the market cross, this time right outside Cohan's Bar. Joe, Gene and the others milled around the doorway to the shop that doubled as the outside of a bar. Under the ever diligent gaze of John Ford they placed a large mattress on the ground beneath the eye-line of the camera.

"I wonder what the mattress is for?" pondered Thomas, as he sat on the ground with his friends on the opposite side of the street.

"Probably for John Wayne when he falls over drunk, I reckon," suggested Michael.

Billy shook his head.

"No, no. It's for when that big feller there gets hit by Wayne and comes flying through the door."

He pointed to a large individual bearing a passing resemblance to Victor McLaglen talking earnestly with Ford.

"How do you know that?"

"Because that big feller there is me Uncle Horace," answered Billy. "He's come all the way from Dublin just to be in the film, and somebody says he looks just like the big feller who's really in the film but the big feller who's really in the film is too old to go throwing himself around, so Uncle Horace is going to throw himself through the door instead."

Thomas shook his head.

"These actors, they're hardly in the film at all. I wonder why they bother sometimes."

Joe turned and gave Thomas a slight wave.

"You're dead lucky, you are, having your sister marry a man from America," said Michael.

"They're not married yet. And if me ma has any say in the matter, I doubt they ever will be."

"Have you got any of that bubble-gum left?"

Thomas dipped into his trouser pocket and retrieved one of

the gum packets.

"Remember, if your ma asks where you got it, I didn't give it to you, right?"

The boys nodded as they stuffed their mouths with the chewy substance, all the more enjoyable since the stuff had been banned by the Bishop of Galway the year before.

Ford continued rehearsing Billy's uncle on the other side of the street as a very tired and emotional Patrick O'Dea stepped out of Ryan's Bar, and made his way down the road, nodding to Thomas and then Joe as he came abreast of Cohan's Bar.

"How do you do, Mr O'Dea?"

"I'm doing fine, Joseph, just fine. Looking forward to working with you on Saturday."

Patrick attempted a small salute, missing the side of his head by miles as he stumbled down the road. Thomas drew his knees up and rested his head between his arms in embarrassment until his father had moved on.

"Okay," barked Ford. "Let's go for a shot."

Uncle Horace entered Cohan's Bar and closed the flimsy door through which he would propel himself backwards at Ford's command. The crew retired to the other side of the camera. Joe watched as Patrick walked unsteadily around the corner to his house, taking a deep breath and drawing himself up to his full height before entering.

Seconds later the silence was shattered by a shriek of hysterical anger followed by the sound of splintering wood as Patrick crashed through the front door, presumably, thought Joe, the result of a well-aimed punch from Mrs Mary O'Dea.

As Patrick slumped semi-conscious to the ground approximately thirty yards away Uncle Horace attempted the self-same trick without the aid of Mary's fist to add power to his flight. Joe found himself standing on the corner looking back and forth between Patrick's house and Cohan's Bar. Seconds after Horace flew through the fake door Ford turned to Joe.

"Well? You're always full of ideas, Mr Yates. What do you think? Another take?"

Joe looked down to where Patrick still lay in the street.

"You really want to know what I think, Mr Ford?" asked Joe amiably.

Ford nodded.

"I think you're filming in the wrong doorway."

Heather returned from work at five to find herself stepping across the shattered woodwork of the front door.

She felt the tension hit her like a jackhammer as she squirmed through the jagged opening into the parlour, a tension Heather had not felt since before her father had left nearly two years ago. The strained atmosphere was heightened further by her mother staring daggers at Heather and her father with equal ferocity.

Thomas sat quietly at the table chewing on a piece of bread and jam, while Patrick sat in the corner nursing a severely bruised jaw. The discord and anger that greeted Heather the minute she entered the house confirmed her desire to be gone from this place as quickly as possible and never to look back.

She looked to Thomas for some indication as to what had happened but he avoided her gaze, just shrugging his shoulders slightly to signal his resignation at the fact that now his father was back it would be just like old times, whether he and his sister liked it or not.

Mary sat at the table and bent her head to pray, obviously not concerned that the rest of the family had yet to join her and Thomas for the evening meal. Heather hung up her coat and sat down to eat, whilst Patrick slowly rose from the chair in the corner to take his place at the end of the table where he had sat the day before.

As he started to sit down Mary thumped the table and froze him with a sharp stare. Patrick took the chair and moved to the side of the table next to Thomas. They ate in silence for a moment or two until Heather could take the strain no longer. She cleared her throat and smiled at her mother.

"Mrs Doonan came into the shop today, mother. She said there was an awful to do over at the church. Something about the font going missing."

Mary ignored her daughter as she continued to pin Patrick to the wall with a murderous glare. Thomas ate even more voraciously than normal if that was possible, looking to Heather and shaking his head quickly to signal that this particular subject was not up for discussion, and pushing his foot sharply against his sister's shin beneath the table to emphasise the point. Heather got the message. A moment later she tried once more to break the repressive hostility that continued to envelop the room.

"Mother, there's a little gathering tonight over at Ryan's Bar. Katherine Donohue tells me Dunphy's managed to get hold of a battery operated wireless and everybody's going to come down to listen to the boxing match, all the way from America. Isn't that exciting?"

Mary snorted as she wiped away the crumbs on the table cloth. Heather pressed on.

"Can I go, please, mother?"

Mary put down her cutlery with a wry grin and finally looked at Heather.

"Can I go, please, mother?" repeated Mary in a cruel impression of her daughter, as she grabbed the edge of the table and leaned towards Heather.

"Such an innocent, such a sweet child," said Mary.

Heather was unsure what to make of the compliments coming her way, until Mary's mouth curled to reveal the hypocrisy of her sentiments.

"You can tell that - that friend of yours - and your father's..." Mary glared at Patrick who visibly flinched. "... Joseph Yates - if I catch him hanging around you like some dog in heat I will personally send him back to where he came from with a tanned behind, do you hear me?"

Heather reacted with equal fury, angry at her mother questioning Joe's intentions towards her.

"What has Joe Yates got to with you?"

"I will not have my daughter gallivanting around the village with some gawk-eared Yank..."

"He is not gawk-eared! He happens to be..."

"He happens to be out for one thing and one thing only. If you're too stupid to see that, my girl, then you will not leave this house until those Hollywood heathens leave us in peace. And the sooner the better as far as I'm concerned."

Heather crossed her arms in defiance and sat back in her chair as Mary continued.

"You stay away from him, do you hear me?"

"I will do nothing of the sort."

"Don't talk to your mother in that tone of voice," interjected Patrick.

"Shut up, you Judas," hissed Mary. Patrick retreated from the fray as Mary resumed the argument with Heather.

"I have it on good authority from Michael Cassidy's mother that your Mr Yates has been boasting to everybody in the village about his girlfriend back in America and how you're just a mere diversion until he gets home."

Heather knew instinctively this was not true. Joe would never do that to her. Such deviousness was totally beyond him, which was one of the many reasons he was so special to her.

"And who told Mrs Cassidy that?"

"Her son, Michael."

"And you believe him? You believe that little insect? Somebody who's been trying to get into my knickers for the last ten years?"

"Don't be so disgusting."

Heather clenched her teeth and bellowed back at her mother.

"Cassidy's a liar. A bloody liar."

Mary whipped her hand across Heather's face, leaving a red welt on her daughter's cheek. Thomas stopped eating. Patrick froze in his chair. Heather slowly rose from her chair, quivering with anger at the thought her own mother would take the word of Michael Cassidy against hers.

"Up until now I could always forgive you for your tantrums, and your wailing and ranting and the way you treat me as though I'm still seven years old but this time, mother, this time you've gone too far."

Heather stepped away from the table.

"Sit down right now," shouted Mary, "or so help me I'll..."

She looked to Patrick for some kind of assistance, but Mary's emasculation of her husband had been too complete, his blank stare signifying that no parental admonition would be forthcoming from him. Heather opened the door leading to the bedroom stairs.

"If either of you think that for one minute I'm going to stay in this village for the rest of my life while the world passes me by then you just don't know me very well. And I don't think you ever will."

Heather left the room, slamming the door behind her.

As darkness fell Heather lay in her bed contemplating how different life might be if she were to go to America with Joe. The more she thought about him the more she realised how much Joe meant to her. At first, if she were honest with herself, she had initially viewed Joe more as a means to an end, a convenient one-way ticket out of Cong, rather than somebody she would contemplate spending her life with. She'd even given some thought to the possibility of maybe realising her ambition to go to college or university to study and make something of herself.

Over the last few days, however, she had come to accept that she would never find anybody as kind, tactful or so lovingly innocent as Joe Yates. And she was not going to let the opportunity to make something of her life with Joe slip through her fingers. Not without a fight, that was for certain, particularly when it came to her mother.

She felt a slight twinge of guilt as it occurred to her that leaving Thomas alone with Mary and Patrick might not be the kindest thing one could do to your own brother, but he'd survive. And he'd be able to get away from this place a damned sight quicker and a lot younger than she had been able to, that's for sure.

As Heather's musings on what the future held for her and Joe became more fanciful, she heard the sound of her mother's footsteps on the creaking stairs followed by a discreet knock on her bedroom door. She closed her eyes as Mary slowly pushed the door ajar and peered in, holding a small candle to illuminate the tiny room, before quietly leaving.

Having heard Thomas go to bed about half an hour before, Heather waited for her father to climb the stairs for bed before making her move. A fully clothed Heather threw back the sheets and opened her window slightly to let in some of the cool evening air. After waiting a further ten minutes or so she knew she was safe as the sound of snoring filtered through the wall from her parent's bedroom. Holding her shoes, Heather opened the door and descended to the parlour as quietly as possible, deftly avoiding the weakest part of the wooden stairs before reaching the bottom step, then making a quick dash out through the back of the house into the night.

Heather could hear the noise coming from Ryan's Bar about a hundred yards away. The loud conversation from the gathering within mingled with what appeared to be a small orchestra playing music from somewhere on the other side of the world. She opened the door cautiously and peered into the bar. The air was thick with tobacco smoke and the pungent smell of freshly brewed beer. The music came from an old battery powered radio, its covering removed to reveal a large collection of wires and glowing valves. Joe sat with Gene and Bo as Gene turned a small dial with the aid of a pocket screwdriver, the music disappearing in a cacophony of high pitched whistling and static as he tried to tune the receiver into the boxing match. Over at the bar sat Wayne and McLaglen, overseeing the distribution of the third round of drinks that evening.

A small cheer rang out from the group by the radio as the sound of the boxing announcer rang out loud and clear from the tiny speaker, Gene waving his hand for quiet as he fine-tuned the receiver. Heather slipped into the bar and leaned against the door, hoping Joe would see her before some busybody enquired as to her presence. She had been in pubs before, but usually only in the company of friends. The tongues would start wagging before she walked through the door, that she knew and accepted. What Heather did not want to encourage was the notion that she frequented the drinking establishments of Cong unescorted. Her mother had enough ammunition as it was.

Concentrating as hard as she could, Heather willed Joe to turn away from the radio and look in her direction. To her surprise and relief he did just that, jumping up from his chair and nearly knocking over a table full of drinks in his delight at seeing her there. Stopping awkwardly in front of her, Joe stooped down to kiss Heather on the cheek, both of them grinning and blushing as they realised that everyone in Ryan's Bar was looking in their direction. Heather returned Joe's kiss with a peck on the cheek then took him by the hand, leading him to a small cubby hole tucked away at the back of the pub half in sight of the main bar. They sat holding hands for a moment or two, neither of them speaking as they basked in the glow of each other's company.

"So. You made it then?" said Joe, stating the obvious.

"Of course. I said I'd be here, didn't I?"

"Your mother? You told her..."

"Mother doesn't mind. She knows where I am. How's the fight going?"

"Sugar Ray Robinson will walk it. Turpin doesn't stand a chance. It's a cinch."

"And how much have you bet on him?"

Joe reacted as if stung.

"Me? Bet? You gotta be kidding. Gambling's for suckers. I'm saving my money for when I get back to the States so I can take flying lessons. I'm gonna be a pilot some day."

"Just saving for flying lessons?"

Her question dangled in the air for a while, Heather lowering her head to catch the reaction on Joe's face. Joe grinned and squeezed her hand.

"And us. You and me, that is."

Heather kissed him on the neck and whispered.

"How about a drink then? To us."

Joe's happiness turned to concern.

"You old enough to drink?" asked Joe.

"Lemonade. With plenty of bubbles."

Joe stood as he put his hand into his pocket for the money.

"One lemonade coming up."

Heather watched as Joe moved to the bar and engaged in the standard ritual for this particular evening which consisted of standing on tiptoe behind the swaying throng at the bar, trying to attract the attention of Dunphy or one of his assistant barmen brought in especially for the occasion. Whilst

Heather's attention was on Joe, Michael Cassidy casually strolled over and leaned against the wooden screen separating Heather from the rest of the pub.

"Heather O'Dea," said Cassidy in mock surprise. "What brings you to this part of the world? Never knew you were the socialising type."

Heather kept her eyes on Joe.

"I choose who I socialise with very carefully," said Heather with equal sarcasm.

"I can see that alright," replied Cassidy, indicating Joe still waiting to be served at the bar. "Local boys not your taste, then? Can't abide them in your dignified presence?"

Cassidy leaned down closer into the snug.

"Stay pure, Miss O'Dea. Stay pure."

Heather jumped up from the table, her quick temper instantly at boiling point. She clenched her fists and raised her voice as loud as she could to be heard over the din of the bar and the ever-increasing volume of the radio announcer excitedly reporting the climax to the boxing match.

"You listen to me, you filthy minded lying little sh…"

As if by magic the noisy cheering suddenly stopped within the bar, causing Heather's voice to carry right across the room. She looked on in embarrassment as Bo and Gene held their heads in their hands.

"I don't believe it," moaned Bo. "Turpin won."

A collective groan arose from the members of the cast and crew. The whole place was suddenly in an uproar, the villagers having placed their bets on Randolph Turpin against the considered opinion of the Yanks who had backed Sugar Ray Robinson to win. Heather found herself looking at a grinning Cassidy who performed a little jig before walking away, just as Joe got back from the bar.

Quinn jumped up and down as he called across to the film crew gathered disconsolately around the now dead radio.

"Fifty-three pounds! Fifty-three pounds. Can you believe it? That's more than I've earned in the last three years. Jesus!"

Gene and Bo were quickly surrounded by a group of enthusiastic villager's eager to count their winnings. McLaglen held out his hand to Wayne who solemnly opened his wallet, pulling out a large wad of pound notes and slapping them heavily into his fellow actor's palm. McLaglen rubbed his hands in delight then joined the loose queue that had formed next to Gene's table to collect his winnings from the bet he had also laid with Bo. Wayne held up his empty wallet, threw back the rest of his drink and sauntered out of the bar. Joe sat with Heather, watching Cassidy noisily slurping his drink as he waited in line for his money.

"I didn't think that guy was a friend of yours. Is he?" said Joe, eyeing Cassidy.

Heather snorted in disgust.

"Good God, no. In fact, he's one of the reasons I'm looking to be out of this place."

Joe turned in pleasant surprise.

"Really?"

"Really."

Gene looked up at the expectant faces crowded around him and counted out the last of his money to Quinn.

"That's it, I'm all out. The rest of you guys are going to have to wait until tomorrow."

He turned to Bo.

"Reckon the old man would bail us out 'til we're Stateside?" asked Gene.

Bo nodded.

"Sure he would. Then he'd spend the rest of our lives reminding us how stupid we were. There has to be another way."

The mood in the pub changed quickly. The exuberance of the gamblers, Cassidy among them, evaporated like the thin wisps of cigarette smoke that hung in the air as they contemplated the prospect of going away empty-handed. A strained silence enveloped the bar.

Gene and the rest of the film crew found themselves suddenly isolated from the villagers. Cassidy spat on the floor in front of Gene.

"Just like a Yank. You come here and take what belongs to

us..." he looked across at Heather then glared at Joe, "...and you don't give any back." Cassidy pointed his glass menacingly at Gene.

"You've got ten seconds to come up with the money, you thieving..."

Cassidy's tirade was cut short as a large wad of bank notes wrapped in three elastic bands flew through the air and landed on Gene's table. All heads moved in one direction to where an awkward-looking Joe stood leaning against the entrance to the snug, his hands in his pockets.

"Settle up with everybody, Gene," mumbled Joe. "Pay me back later."

Gene gave Joe a grateful slap on the back then disappeared beneath a crush of people as he started to dish out the money. Heather put her hand on Joe's arm, standing on tiptoe as she breathed into his ear.

"I have to go. Walk me home the long way."

Joe drank his beer so fast the liquid never even touched the sides of his throat.

Joe happily let Heather lead him away from the centre of the village, figuring that their route through the dark streets would eventually take them around the outskirts of Cong and back to her house. They walked hand-in-hand for awhile until Joe plucked up enough courage to put his arm around her shoulders, holding Heather close to keep her warm. They continued strolling in silence. Joe looked up into the night sky.

"No moon."

"No matter. We don't need any light tonight."

She stopped, turned to Joe and kissed him passionately. He nearly jumped six feet as her tongue made contact with his. He'd heard of that kind of kissing before, but none of the girls he had ever kissed back in the States kissed like that. Not even on a third date. Heather pulled away and took Joe's hand.

"How much longer are you here for?" she asked as they resumed their walk.

Joe was now very weak at the knees in anticipation of being kissed in the same fashion again, and tried to collect his thoughts.

"Uh, let me see. Today's… uh..."

"Tuesday."

"Yep, Tuesday, that's right, Tuesday and… uh..."

"Tomorrow's Wednesday."

"Sure, tomorrow's Wednesday and… I guess a few more weeks unless we're told otherwise. Tomorrow we're off to Bally… Bally somewhere... Could we maybe do that kissing thing..."

"Ballyglunin?"

Joe collected his breath. "Ballyglunin. We're going to be there probably all day to do a few shots at the railway station. Then we're back here to do the fight down at the farm. That leaves a couple more courting scenes with Duke and Maureen O'Hara then that's about it. We're pretty much on schedule and the old man..."

"The man at the church the other day? The one who shouts all the time?"

"You got it in one. John Ford. The director. The omnipotent one. The guy who screams all the time. We call him the old man. Wayne calls him Pappy. And a few other things besides. Anyway, he's real happy about the way things have worked out here but he just can't wait to get back to Hollywood and start shooting the interiors."

"Why is he in such a hurry to get back?"

"Reckons he's more at home in a studio. Things don't go wrong all the time."

"So, where do you come from, Joe?"

"Cleveland."

"Is that near Hollywood?

"No, it's miles away. I just drifted down to California one day and got myself a job as a gofer."

Joe saw a quizzical look on Heather's face.

"You know, go for this, go for that. Anyway I'm planning to save enough and - here I am in Ireland. And it's so dark I can't see my hand in front of my face. We're not lost, are we?"

There was more than a hint of expectation in Joe's voice,

hoping that maybe Heather might kiss him again.

"No, we're not lost."

Joe stopped walking, his whole body trembling as he tightened his hold on Heather's hand and pulled her towards him through the darkness. Trying hard to catch his breath Joe wrapped his arms around her and enveloped Heather in a passionate embrace, the intensity of their feelings for each other pushing their bodies close together.

Their lips met, softly at first, she not resisting as he almost lifted her from the ground in his eagerness to taste the sweetness of her mouth. Heather placed her hands on Joe's shoulders and pulled away slightly to get her breath.

"Oh, Joe."

"I know," he gasped. "We'd better stop before..."

"You do and I'll kill you."

She wrapped her arms around his neck and crushed his mouth onto hers. As they kissed and stroked each other Joe fought to keep his libido in gentlemanly check, in the process accidentally brushing Heather across her chest. As they pushed their bodies together Joe managed to trap his hand against her left breast.

His hand automatically recoiled, waiting for the inevitable slap around the face that had normally followed such a faux pas as this in the past. But to his amazement and increasing delight, no such reaction was forthcoming. He tentatively cupped Heather's breast once more, her nipple hardening beneath his touch, the promise of that moment almost too much for Joe to bear. They stood in the darkness, neither of them knowing what to do next, but both of them very sure of where this was all going to lead if they both desired. After a moment Heather took Joe's hand and kissed it.

"Joe, you're such a gentleman. What am I going to do with you?"

They held each other once more. Joe looked down at her face, the outline of Heather's features becoming more pronounced as his eyes got used to the dark.

"God, you're so beautiful."

"Only beautiful?"

They started to walk on back towards the village, managing to get their breathing under control. At the end of the road leading to Heather's house stood a gas lamp beneath which they held each other once more. Joe kissed her again.

"How's that? Better than the other night?"

"Mmmmm. I think you're getting the hang of it."

Joe looked into her eyes.

"Yates. Joe and Heather Yates," he mused as Heather rested her head on his chest. "We could marry in Cleveland then…"

She suddenly pulled away.

"You stop right there, Mr Joseph Yates," she declared angrily to a bewildered Joe.

"I like you right enough but don't you start getting any fancy ideas that I'm going to uproot myself and leave my family the minute one of you Yanks flashes a smile at me. Cleveland? You can't be serious now, can you?"

"I thought you wanted to get out of this place. With me. We're going steady, aren't we? I mean… I like you. I do. Really."

"But do you love me, Mr Yates? Do you love me enough that you would want to take me away from my family, my home? Drag me off to a strange land where I'll probably be looked upon as some sort of novelty by your cousins in Cleveland or California or wherever it is you come from? Do you?"

Joe tried to hold her again as she stepped away, his empty arms flailing at the air.

"Come on, don't be sore. I want to take you away from here, sure I do. If you'll come I guess."

Heather stood her distance.

"I love you. That's… what more can I say? I love you."

Heather looked up and smiled, moving closer.

"Well, that's fine then. We'll get married, settle down, have lots of children."

Joe held out his open arms to welcome her into his arms once more.

"Here. In Ireland," she added. Heather knew she was playing a dangerous game with Joe and would give anything to leave the village at that moment with him and never look back.

More than that, though, she needed to know that Joe's love for her was real and the only way Joe could prove his intentions were genuine was to agree to stay in Ireland with her. Even if that was the last thing she wanted.

Unfortunately for Heather, living in Ireland wasn't in Joe's grand plan. "Now, hold on there just a minute. I'm not too sure I want to spend the rest of my life in a place like..."

Heather hid her disappointment and laughed bitterly.

"So then, Joseph Yates, we know the depth of your commitment towards your intended now, don't we? Well let me tell you something. You want me, you can have me. But on my terms. Do not take me for granted. I'm Irish, and I wish to stay in Ireland. If you really feel the way you do about me, then you'll stay here too. Who knows, you might even get to like it. Goodnight."

She moved out of the light and ran off towards her house before Joe could stop her. He thought of calling out or running after her, but he instinctively knew that would only make matters worse. The last thing he wanted was a shouting match in the middle of the village at night. He forlornly watched her fade from his sight, wondering what he had done to deserve such a lambasting. Somebody should publish a handbook, he thought to himself as he walked sorrowfully off into the night, some kind of guide or manual on how to behave when it came to being with a woman. They'd make a million.

Heather tiptoed into the house and made her way across the parlour towards the staircase door. Her mother's voice shot out of the darkness like an arrow, stopping her daughter in her tracks and causing Heather's heart to thud in shock. She turned to see Mary silhouetted against the window with her back to her.

"Did you see him again?" asked Mary.

"Yes, I saw him. You shouldn't fret, mother. It's nothing. It's not what you think."

"And what do I think?"

"You think the worst, mother. You always think the worst."

She started to walk up the stairs.

"Heather…"

Mary's plaintive voice pulled her daughter back into the room.

"He'll leave. Just like your father did. And you'll end up like me. Standing in the dark with nobody to hold."

Heather walked over to her mother.

"But he's back now. He's back and he's here, in this house. With us. With you." Heather crossed her fingers, hoping this might counteract any notion her father might have of abandoning the family home in the near future.

"I know. But for how long?"

Mary lowered her head and cried softly. Heather put her arms around her mother's shoulder as Mary slowly regained her composure.

"Go on, now, get to bed. It's late."

"How about you?"

"Later. Later."

Heather took one last look at her mother as she continued to stare out into the bleakness of the night. No future daughter of hers would ever have to look upon such a scene of misery as the one that confronted her now.

CHAPTER SEVEN

The clouds came out the day they went to Ballyglunin, which happened to suit Joe's frame of mind right down to the ground. Ford cursed the intemperate weather and all things Irish as he contemplated where to put the camera in order to eliminate the grey cloud-strewn sky from the frame. The scene called for a train to enter the station from which Wayne's character Sean Thornton would alight, a sequence that would actually be used at the beginning of the film, despite the fact the crew had already been shooting for five weeks. As Ford discussed camera angles with his cinematographer, Joe tapped Gene on the shoulder and pointed to a bridge spanning both platforms.

"Hey, Gene. Why doesn't he put the camera up on the bridge? He'd get a great shot of the train coming into the station and he could cut out the sky at the same time."

Gene shook his head and smiled, pulling his empty pockets out of his trousers.

"As you can see, I have no money. Although I promise the minute we hit the States... I swear on my mother's grave, you'll get back every penny, I promise..."

"Yeah, yeah, okay. I get the picture. What's that got to do with putting the camera up on the bridge?"

"I was going to bet you money that you wouldn't go ask Ford the same question."

Joe shuddered.

"Damned right I wouldn't. Think I'm crazy or something? Let him chew somebody else's ass out. Mine's down to the bone."

Gene turned to his friend with a look of concern.

"Kinda tetchy today, ain't we? What's wrong?"

Joe blew out his cheeks in frustration.

"Nothing a trip back home wouldn't cure."

"I thought you liked it here. What about that girl of yours? We all figured you and her were real strong by now."

"You figured wrong. Now tell me...what's the problem with putting the camera up there on the bridge?"

Gene sighed.

"Watch. And listen."

Gene walked over to Ford and coughed slightly, interrupting the director and his cameraman.

"Can I help you?" asked Ford brusquely.

Gene pointed to the bridge further down the platform.

"Me and some of the boys, Mr Ford, we were thinking, maybe you might want to consider putting the camera up there on the bridge, take a shot of the train coming into the station from above. That way you can miss out all these clouds and such."

"You and some of the boys, huh?"

"Yes sir."

"Tell me, Mister Willis. Whenever you speak to somebody, do you make sure you're standing on a ladder first?"

"Never, Mr Ford."

"Do you lie down then look up at them before conversing? Or do you stand and look them straight in the eye?"

"I look at them right between the eyes."

"And that, Mister Willis," Ford declared testily, "is how I shoot motion pictures. So if you don't mind, I'll keep the camera down here on the platform where it can see the train arrive, providing that's alright with you and the boys that is."

Gene conjured enough of a sheepish look to convince Ford that he had seen the error of his ways, backing away as Ford and the cameraman resumed their conversation. He walked towards Joe and a bemused crowd of onlookers including Wayne who had gathered to witness the exchange between him and Ford. Gene bowed slightly to his audience.

"Gentlemen. Here endeth the lesson."

Wayne lit a cigarette and took Joe and Gene to one side.

"You ought to know by now, Gene. Pappy's always right..."

"Even when he's wrong," chorused Gene and Joe.

"You gonna tell him otherwise?" queried Wayne.

Joe shrugged.

"Not in so many words. But surely a director ought to take chances every now and then, break a few of the rules? I mean, audiences go to the movies to see a movie, not a film of a script. Otherwise they may as well go watch a play."

Ford called out to Wayne before the actor could respond.

"I'm on. Gene. Tell Joe here about the time Ford crossed the line."

Wayne wandered off up the platform to confer with Ford.

"What's he mean, crossed the line?"

"Ever see Stagecoach?"

"Of course I have. Best western ever made."

Gene looked over his shoulder towards Ford.

"You obviously haven't seen Red River."

"The old man didn't direct Red River, did he? I thought Howard Hawks..."

"Sshhh," whispered Gene. "In Stagecoach, remember the Indian chase when Duke sat on top of the coach shooting everybody just before the cavalry arrived?"

"Uh huh."

"Okay. Now when you film a moving object you either shoot it going from the left of the screen to the right or vice versa, depending upon the direction of the action. Understand?"

"Yeah, I understand, I understand," said Joe, not too sure what Gene was getting at but nodding anyway.

"Now, should you film a moving object such as a stagecoach going from left to right, then cut away and come back to the same moving object going from right to left then you end up confusing the audience, because now they don't know which way the stagecoach is travelling."

"Right, okay," replied Joe. "So you make sure you only ever

film it going in one direction, right?"

"Absolutely. No director worth their salt ever crosses the line of action otherwise you end up distracting the concentration of the audience. Make sense?"

"So far. So what are you saying? Ford broke the rules and crossed the line?"

"Yep. Not only that but nobody even noticed when he did it."

"How come?" asked Joe with genuine interest.

"Easy," replied Gene with a hint of triumph. "He filmed it in one continuous take. First off he shot the stagecoach going left to right then he drove the camera truck across the front of the stagecoach and filmed it going right to left, and nobody even realised what he'd done. He broke one of the first rules of movie-making and the audience didn't notice goddam thing."

Gene could see that Joe was impressed.

"Which only goes to prove, Joseph my boy, why that son-of-a-bitch is probably the greatest director that ever lived."

He put a friendly arm around Joe's shoulder.

"Anyway, enough about that old galoot. Now. What's the problem between you and that girl of yours? Tell Uncle Gene everything."

Back at the village Heather was just about to go for lunch when Patrick suddenly darted into the shop, glancing behind him as if he were being followed. He closed the door and approached his daughter with genuine contrition.

"I think you and I need to have a conversation."

"What about? You've been back nearly a week and only now you decide maybe we should talk?"

Patrick nodded to Gallagher as he appeared from the store room. Gallagher acknowledged Patrick in return.

"Good day, Patrick. Heather, I'm off down to the bank for about half an hour."

Patrick drummed his fingers on the counter as he left. After a few moments of strained silence Heather finally lost her patience.

"Look, there's nothing you can say to me that's going to make up for you leaving us like you did so don't bother. Besides, if you should be talking to anybody then it ought to be ma, not me."

"She won't listen. She doesn't want to know."

Heather leaned against the counter which separated her from Patrick.

"I'm not surprised. How could you? Selling the font. What on earth did you think you were up to?"

Patrick held up his arms in a gesture of supplication.

"I wanted to be the man of the house again. I wanted to bring home the bread like I'm supposed to."

"So what did you do with the money you got for the font?"

"I drank it, of course. A man has to be able to buy a round. Otherwise I'd never be able to hold my head up. I have my pride, you know."

Heather decided not to even bother attempting to follow his warped logic. He was set in his ways and nothing she could say or do would ever change that. Silence descended between the two once more.

"So," said Patrick finally, "you and this Joe feller. Is it as serious as your mother seems to think?"

"What's it to you, anyway?"

Patrick's eyes flashed with anger.

"I may not be the best father in the world, young lady, but don't you dare to speak to me in that tone of voice. Not unless you want me to come round that counter and take my belt off to you."

Heather looked away, trying hard to contain the anger she felt towards her father. She failed, the bitterness dripping from every word that she threw Patrick's way.

"Oh, that's just wonderful. You walk out two years ago on your own wife and two children without even saying goodbye, leaving me to help fend and provide for your family - your family - then you traipse back here as though you've never been gone and what do you say? Sorry? Forgive me? I didn't mean to do it and I know I was wrong?"

Patrick stood in the centre of the shop, his head bowed. Heather lifted up the counter, slamming it down behind her as she stood in front of her father. She folded her arms and rocked from side to side in anger, dropping her voice to a low, menacing whisper.

"You have the gall to walk in off the street back into our lives as if you've never been away, then threaten me with the belt. Let me tell you something, father. You don't have the right. Not anymore. You threw away your claim on us the day you walked out. I'm the breadwinner of this family. I'm the one who had to plead with Mr Gallagher to give me a job so we could all eat. I'm the one who fed and clothed everybody in your absence and no amount of beatings or whippings with your trouser belt is going to change that."

Heather wiped the tears from her face with the back of her hand.

Patrick started to say something, before appearing to think better of it. He moved towards the door, turning to face Heather at the same time.

Patrick spoke in a hushed tone, his voice betraying the sadness he felt at the yawning gulf that separated him from his daughter.

"You know, yesterday, when you and your mother argued, after you left the room, she said how much you reminded her of me. And in a way she's right. I'm not stupid. I can tell you want to get out of here as much as I did. Nobody can blame you for that, least of all me. But you know, Heather, standing here right now, listening to you throwing all this back in my face, I close my eyes and I see her. In you. I hear her. In you. And I thank you, I truly do."

"You thank me?"

Patrick opened the door and stepped out into the light.

"Yes, Heather, I thank you. For reminding me why I left."

Heather involuntarily reached out to her father as he closed the door behind him, her tears staining the glass as she pressed her face against the door. A dull hollow ache welled up inside her as she watched her father shuffle across the road towards Ryan's Bar, her anger all but dissipated at the sight of having watched him age nearly ten years in a matter of moments. She knew that if she did not call out to him now the moment would be lost for ever and her father with it.

Patrick stood outside Ryan's slapping his jacket pockets in the hope he might disturb enough loose change to purchase the amount of alcohol required in order to anaesthetise the pain of the last few minutes. Finding a few silver coins in his trouser pocket, he was about to enter the pub when a voice called out to him from across the road, a voice softer and more restrained than the one he had been subjected to moments before.

"Father?"

Patrick wheeled round to face his daughter, expecting further invective and ill-feeling to come flying his way.

"Can I buy you a drink?" she asked, joining him on the other side of the road.

Patrick frowned, not knowing how to react to Heather's change in attitude. Luckily his thirst decided the matter for him.

"Are you sure you're old enough to be drinking, young lady?"

"You ought to know that," she said. "After all, you are my father."

CHAPTER EIGHT

The scenes in Ballyglunin took nearly two days to complete, which was a day longer than Ford had anticipated. This meant he was even more surly than normal when the crew finally arrived back in Cong to continue filming. It was also why he was in no mood to indulge anybody, not even John Wayne, when it came to spending free time in Ryan's Bar in the evenings.

Although accommodation had been booked for a solid three months in and around Cong, Ford was anxious to get back to the States and wrap the whole thing up. Confident that he could get everything he needed in the can by the following Monday at the latest, Ford decided to cut the original shooting schedule in half, which meant Joe and the others would be leaving six weeks earlier than originally intended.

Joe ached to be with Heather again, to try and work things out between them before he left. But the tight shooting schedule meant that he was not able to get back into Cong until at least two days after returning from Ballyglunin. And the circumstances under which Joe found himself back in the village were not particularly auspicious, to say the least.

One week before shooting was due to finish, and three days before the celebrations to welcome electricity to the village were to take place, Thomas was in his room reading his John

Wayne comic for the twentieth time, when he was distracted by the sound of small stones tapping against the window. He looked out into the street to see Michael and Billy standing outside the house. Opening the window Thomas leaned out and put his finger to his mouth, indicating to his friends not to make any noise. Michael whispered loudly to his friend.

"What are you doing in your room? It's nearly the afternoon."

"Me ma's said I can't go out until they've finished making the film and they've all left the village."

"But we're in the fight scene tomorrow. Is she not letting you go?"

"Da's persuaded her we can still go by telling her he'll give her all the money he gets as an extra but that's all she's agreed I can do. So right now I'm stuck in here."

Michael cupped his hand to his mouth.

"John Wayne's over at Ryan's Bar. He and some boxer feller. They've gone and got themselves drunk. There's a big crowd outside the place waiting to see what's going to happen. You've got to come and see this."

Thomas weighed up his options, decided he might never get the chance to set eyes on his hero again, and concluded nothing his mother could do to him would be worse than that.

"Wait around the corner for me. I'll be down in a minute."

Thomas and his friends hurried through the village and joined the crowd gathered just across the street from Ryan's Bar. Thomas tried to get a better look at the proceedings through the legs of Vincent Corrigan, Gerald O'Brien and Michael Cassidy who stood on the edge of the crowd, everyone awaiting the inevitable eruption of violence within. Wayne's voice rang out loud and clear through a half-open window.

"Come on, Thornton, put up your fists. I can take you anytime I want. Only one of us is gonna walk out of here."

O'Brien announced his ignorance to the crowd.

"Who's Thornton when he's at home?"

"Where have you been for the last ten years?" replied Vincent. "Mairtin Thornton. 'Marching' Mairtin Thornton. Irish professional heavyweight. Full time thug."

"Good," said O'Brien. "Let's hope he massacres the living daylights out of that Hollywood fake."

Another voice rang out from inside the bar, a voice tinged with a heavy Irish accent and a not inconsiderable amount of alcohol.

"Duke. Duke. You'll be looking after me if I go to Hollywood, isn't that so?"

"Course I will, Thornton," replied Wayne, his voice less slurred than those of his companion. "Only you and me, we've gotta settle something right here first."

Thomas tensed with the rest of the crowd, expecting to hear

the sound of a crunching fist upon yielding flesh at any moment. A breathless Joe appeared from the direction of Ashford Castle, running his hands through his hair as he pushed open the door to Ryan's.

Thomas bit his lip and turned to his friends.

"Looks like me sister's gonna be a widder before she even gets hitched."

Silence descended as everyone strained to hear the conversation from inside the bar. Joe's tremulous voice cut through the air.

"Uh... Mr Wayne... er... sir, uh... Mr Ford would like the pleasure of your company back at Ashford Castle. Uh... immediately, sir, if you please, that is, I..."

As Wayne's voice boomed out in response, Thomas caught sight of Michael Cassidy with a big grin on his face and punching his fist into the palm of his hand.

No doubt waiting for Joe to get a good hiding, thought Thomas.

"You can tell Mr Ford from me, sonny, I ain't going nowhere," bellowed Wayne. "I'm having me a damned good time right here in Cong. Ain't that right, Thornton?"

"It is, Duke, it is. Now, I'd consider it an honour if you'd let me punch the lights out on this young whippersnapper. Is that okay with you?"

"No," said Wayne. Thomas saw the smile drop from Cassidy's

face. "Leave him be," continued Wayne. "He's a good kid, just doing his job, that's all."

The crowd moved back as the door to Ryan's swung open, Joe leaving first with Wayne and Thornton staggering close behind. The villagers suddenly looked in every direction but the one that had commanded their attention only seconds before. Cassidy walked off down the road with slumped shoulders, whilst O'Brien and Corrigan made their way to Hanratty's. Thomas said goodbye to Michael and Billy. Heather appeared from around the corner as she walked back from the house after her lunch break just as Joe, Wayne and Thornton made off towards Ashford Castle. She wagged her finger and lightly scolded her younger brother.

"What are you doing here? You're supposed to be at home. Mother will knock you into next week if you're not careful."

"I had to come. It sounded like Wayne was going to punch the living daylights out of Joe."

"Joe? What happened?" gasped Heather involuntarily.

"I didn't think you were interested any more," said her brother.

"I'm not, He can get beat up for all I care," she said, stomping up the street towards Gallagher's.

Thomas smiled. Joe would get the girl in the end, he thought to himself. Anybody who took on John Wayne and lived deserved that much at least.

CHAPTER NINE

The sun shone brightly the following day when Ford came to shoot the final scenes for the climactic fight between John Wayne's character, Sean Thornton, and Victor McLaglen, who was playing the part of Maureen O'Hara's brother, Red Will Danaher.

Everybody standing behind the camera prayed the weather would stay that way as the director gave instructions to Wayne and O'Hara for the first set-up of the day. Everybody apart from Joe. Joe wanted cloud, lots of it. Enough to delay the shooting of the rest of the film while he tried to patch things up with Heather. The sun had other ideas, taunting Joe as it evaded any cloud that dared to obscure its defiant glare.

A crowd of extras including Patrick O'Dea, Thomas and his friends stood on the rise of a hill behind the two main stars awaiting their cue. Ford nodded to to his assistant director who then turned to the extras.

"Okay," said the AD through cupped hands, "you know what to do. We're going for a shot."

"Roll it," said Ford.

Wayne grabbed O'Hara by the top of her arm and started to pull her roughly behind him, the extras baying and shouting as they followed the warring couple down into the meadow.

A woman ran out of the crowd and proffered a large stick to Wayne.

"Here's a stick to beat the nice lady with," said the female extra.

"There'll be hell to pay when the Irish see that," whispered Gene to no one in particular.

"Cut!" said Ford. "That's fine."

At the top of a hill above the meadow stood a number of props including an old-fashioned threshing machine and a blacksmith's boiler. The crew moved the camera and lights up the hill next to the boiler, with the intention of shooting the initial confrontation between Wayne and Victor McLaglen. McLaglen himself stood on the hill with some of the other actors waiting for the shot to be set up.

Although Heather was still uppermost in Joe's mind, his concentration had been directed most of the morning towards shifting equipment to and fro across the meadow. His hopes soared skywards when he saw Patrick and Thomas in the crowd, figuring that Heather might not be too far away. Taking a breather for a moment, Joe approached the extras.

"Uh… Mr O'Dea?"

Patrick stood with his arm around his son's shoulder. He greeted Joe warmly, shaking him by the hand.

"This film-making lark, it's enough to test a man's thirst with all this waiting around." said Patrick.

"Mr Ford usually gets it right first time. We should be finished in a couple of hours."

An awkward silence descended between the two men.

"Is Heather coming over today?" asked Joe hopefully.

"I couldn't tell you, Joe, but I know one thing for sure, she's been in a devil of a mood for the last week or so and that's the truth. Everything alright between you two?"

Joe looked to the ground and put his hands in his pocket as always whenever he had difficulty expressing himself.

Ford's commanding voice cut through the air before Joe was able to stutter a response.

"Wait a minute! Come back and put the camera here," he ordered the crew. "Duke, Maureen, I wanna try something."

Patrick sighed.

"What's he up to now? Stopping and starting like this. We'll be here into next week. I'm waiting to see Wayne and McLaglen have at it."

"The old man must have come up with something new," said Joe.

He shielded his eyes against the sun as he scanned the meadow, hoping with all of his heart that Heather might suddenly appear. But she was nowhere to be seen.

Wayne and O'Hara conferred with Ford as he gave them new instructions. The director then turned to his AD, who stood a respectful distance away and waved at him to join them. After a moment the AD walked across to the extras and addressed the crowd.

"Okay, we're shooting a new scene here. Just stay back like you did before, then move forward along with Mr Wayne and Miss O'Hara as they make their way towards the top of the hill. And Joe?"

Joe looked at the AD in surprise and pointed to himself, his thoughts still on the absent Heather.

"Me?"

"Yeah, you, Joe. You're supposed to be behind the camera, not in front of it. Come on, before the old man sees you. It's my ass too, you know."

"Sorry."

Joe stepped away from the crowd and placed himself out of shot. The AD nodded to Ford that the extras were now in position.

"Action!" growled Ford.

Wayne and O'Hara resumed their tug of war, this time O'Hara losing a shoe as Wayne pulled her along.

Ford pointed at one of the extras at the front of the crowd.

"Pick the shoe up! Pick it up and give it to her."

The extra ran forward and handed the shoe to O'Hara. As she tried to put it back on the actress over-balanced and fell to the ground. Wayne grabbed the collar of her jacket and yanked her across the meadow, making it look from a distance as though he had hold of O'Hara by her hair. The actress then struggled to her feet and swung her fist towards Wayne's head. In a perfectly choreographed move, Wayne ducked and the momentum of O'Hara's missed punch caused her to end up facing the other way. Wayne finished the scene with a well-aimed kick to the actress' backside.

"Cut!" said a plainly delighted Ford. The extras came to a halt, most of the men including Patrick laughing at the shenanigans of Wayne and O'Hara. The women in the crowd kept their opinions to themselves.

"Here's your fighting partner, Joe" Thomas cried out as Heather wandered down into the meadow. A wide grin spread across Joe's face as Heather made her way in the sunlight towards him. He opened his arms in greeting but she walked right past him, as if oblivious to his presence. Heather stood with hands on hips in front of her father and Thomas.

"I've been watching the fun from up there for the last few minutes," she said, indicating a cluster of trees at the back of the meadow. "A fine example you're setting young Thomas here, father. He'll grow up thinking all men can treat their womenfolk any way they want and get away with it too."

A few murmurs of assent rippled through the crowd from some of the female extras.

"It's only a movie, Heather, it's not for real," said Joe, desperate to elicit some kind of response from her, even it were to be argumentative. Heather ignored him, although her answer acknowledged his presence.

"It's the principle of the thing," she said as she continued to stare at her father. "Thousands, millions of people are going to see this film and go away with the idea that the Irish are a bunch of ignorant peasants who like nothing better than to drag their women round by the hair. Thomas is too young to know better but you, father, you should be ashamed to be a part of this."

Patrick grinned sheepishly.

"Heather, like Joe says, it's only a film. Besides, they're paying Thomas and me good money..."

"They're paying us too, da?" asked Thomas. "How much are they paying us, da, how much?"

"Ssshh, Thomas. Later now, later."

Joe stood in front of Heather.

"Listen to me, please, there's something..."

She cut him dead with a cold stare.

"Let's see what happens next, shall we? Let's see how these fine boys from Hollywood ridicule the Irish further, in the name of entertainment."

She walked away and placed herself in the middle of the crowd. Joe looked at her retreating figure in resignation before loping back up the hill to where Ford and the crew were busy readying the equipment for the next set-up.

Ford took another hour to shoot a number of reaction shots of Victor McLaglen watching the arrival of Wayne and O'Hara down below in the meadow, before taking a break for lunch. The extras swarmed around the refreshment wagon as Joe scouted the edge of the crowd in a vain attempt to catch Heather's attention. Heather had no intention of talking or communicating with Joe further, keeping her eyes firmly fixed on a point above his head whenever Joe came into view. Gene pulled his miserable friend aside.

"Come on, Joe, you're just making things worse for yourself. You keep wandering round in a circle like some kind of gormless idiot. Give it up as a bad job or you're gonna go crazy. Anyway we're going back to the States next week. Forget her." Gene lowered his voice. "Cheer up and maybe I'll introduce you to my cousin."

"Your cousin?" replied Joe, still looking at Heather over by the refreshment truck. "You mean the one with the lazy eye and the limp?"

"She don't limp so bad anymore. Besides, what's wrong with an all-American girl anyway? You could do worse," he nodded towards a stony-faced Heather.

Joe turned to his friend.

"Look, Gene, I appreciate your friendship, I really do but this is something I've got to figure out by myself. I have to work this one out on my own. Okay?"

"Okay, kid, it's your life. But if you ask me..."

Joe held up his hand to signal the discussion was at an end. The AD suddenly clapped his hands loudly.

"Alright, listen up everybody, Mr Ford wants to shoot a few more scenes up by the thresher while the light is still good. If you'll take your positions back at the bottom of the hill, I'll let you know when we're ready for the first shot."

The extras shuffled down into the meadow, Heather staying in the middle of the crowd well away from Joe.

Wayne and O'Hara stood at the bottom of the hill waiting for their cue. Ford had someone bring him his canvas chair which he now occupied in its usual place next to the camera. As the sun momentarily hid behind a small cloud, Ford chewed for a few seconds on his handkerchief. The actors, crew and extras all looked expectantly to the sky. A moment later the sun peeked out from behind the cloud, bathing the meadow in a golden glow.

"Action!"

Wayne moved forward and clamped his hand around O'Hara's wrist as they climbed the hill, the extras milling close behind. Ford's AD suddenly turned to Ford and whispered in his ear.

"Cut," barked Ford, still sitting in his chair. Wayne and O'Hara looked behind them as the director pointed down into the crowd.

"That her?" asked Ford, indicating Heather.

The AD nodded. As one, they both turned and regarded Joe in stony silence. Joe looked around him for a clue as to what he had done to incur Ford's wrath.

"Joe. You in control of the extras or not?" demanded the AD. Joe nodded.

"Sure. Sure I am. Hired them all myself, just like you asked. What's the problem?" Ford stood and pointed down into the meadow.

"My assistant director informs me your girlfriend was not in the last scene we shot, therefore she cannot be in this one." said Ford in a loud voice for the benefit of all to hear.

Joe's ears turned red as Ford addressed him further.

"Continuity, Mr Yates, it's called continuity, one of the most basic rules of film-making. I would be most appreciative if you were to take yourself down into the crowd and remove the young lady, so that maybe we might get a decent shot before we lose the light once more. What do you say?"

Joe wasn't sure whether to laugh or cry. On the one hand he found himself almost wanting to be physically sick now that he was yet once again the target of Ford's wounding sarcasm. However, the elation he felt at being ordered by Ford to retrieve Heather from the crowd was nearly too much for him to bear.

Still, he thought to himself as he made his way down the hill, when Mr Ford says move then you move, no use trying to argue. A strange little smile played across Joe's face as he walked past Wayne and O'Hara, Wayne's obvious look of confusion increasing further as Joe winked to his puzzled friend.

Joe walked confidently through the crowd towards Heather, the extras parting either side of him. She moved away instinctively as he took her lightly by the arm.

"I'm sorry, Miss O'Dea, but Mr Ford says you can't be in the shot. Let's go."

She shook his hand away, embarrassed at being shown up in front of the other villagers.

"I don't want to be in your stupid film anyway."

"That's fine because they don't want you in it either," he said, grabbing her by the wrists and heaving her over his shoulder.

Patrick patted his son on the head as Joe carried his struggling daughter out of the crowd.

"He's gone and got himself a real handful there," mused Patrick. "Just like her mother, she is."

Joe wandered past Wayne and O'Hara as Heather pounded his back with her flailing fists.

"Hi Duke, Miss O'Hara," said Joe as he strolled up the hill, Heather's face now red with embarrassment as well as anger.

"Hi, Joe," replied Wayne with a big grin across his face. Maureen O'Hara bit her lip and looked the other way.

Joe was gasping for breath by the time he reached the top of the hill, throwing Heather unceremoniously onto one of the small haystacks gathered behind the camera.

"Stay there and don't move." warned Joe. He turned to Ford and the waiting crew, giving the director a thumbs-up sign to indicate that he now had the matter firmly under control. Ford and the others watched in bemusement as Heather pushed herself off the haystack and, balling her fist, prepared to deliver a blinding smack to an unsuspecting Joe.

"Don't you dare treat me like that, you..."

"Hey. You," shouted Ford, stopping Heather in mid-swing. "Quiet on my set."

Heather stood with her fist in the air, inches away from Joe's face, her anger now diverging from the idiot boy in front of her towards the old man over by the camera. Joe put his finger to his lips for silence, enraging her even more. Heather let out a strangled cry of frustration then turned away from Joe. Ford sat in his canvas chair, taking one last look behind him to make sure Heather's anger was spent before he resumed filming.

"And - action!" he cried, spurring Wayne and O'Hara into life. As they reached the crest of the hill, Wayne yanked O'Hara in front of him, looking beyond the camera at Victor McLaglen.

"Dannaher. You owe me three hundred and fifty pounds. I want it."

"I'll pay you... Never."

On cue Wayne threw O'Hara onto the ground.

"That breaks all bargains. Take your sister back. It's your custom, not mine. No fortune, no marriage. Let's call it quits."

A tearful O'Hara got to her feet and faced Wayne, brushing the grass from her long skirt.

"You'd do this? To me - after..."

"It's over," growled Wayne.

McLaglen reached into his pocket and retrieved a bundle of money from his wallet.

"There's your filthy money," cried McLaglen, throwing the bundle of notes to his opponent. "Take it and count it, you spawn. And look here," he added, brandishing his fist. "If ever I see that face of yours again I'll push this through it."

Wayne picked up the money then moved towards the blacksmith's boiler. O'Hara opened up the metal door, Wayne threw the money into the fire then O'Hara slammed the door shut.

"Cut!" said Ford. "That was good." The assistant director looked to Ford who gave him a slight nod. The AD called to the extras gathered on the hill.

"Okay. Now we're going to go for the reverse shots before the light starts to fade. Please keep your positions as best you can. Thank you."

Joe turned as Heather pushed her way past the crew and made her way back down into the meadow.

"Thank you for your understanding, young lady," muttered Ford as she stomped past the director. A mournful Joe stood with his hands in his pockets waiting for the inevitable tirade from the old man as Ford walked up to him, puffing on his pipe.

"You like her?"

Joe watched as Heather walked off into the distance, the sunlight caressing her hair as she bounced across the brightly lit meadow before disappearing from view.

"I love her," said Joe.

Ford struck a match and fired up his pipe once more.

"Then what are you waiting for? This is only a movie."

He pointed at the equipment and crew milling around before nodding towards Heather.

"That's the real thing. Don't let it go. Not without a fight."

Patrick lay on the side of the hill, chewing on a piece of grass and shaking his head in clear disappointment.

"Did you see that?" he asked Thomas and his two friends. "Duke Wayne. He threw all the money into the fire. He should be ashamed of himself."

"It's not real money, da. It's only make believe, honest."

"I know that, son, I'm not stupid. But it's the principle of the thing. What a waste."

Joe flashed past Patrick and the extras in pursuit of Heather.

"That boy's making a rod to break his own back. That he certainly is."

Heather wandered across the Rose Cottage bridge and looked down into the clear water of the River Cong, her anger and humiliation slowly carried away by the calming influence of her surroundings. As she stared at her reflection on top of the winding stream, Joe's face suddenly appeared next to hers.

"Hi," he said, waving at the water. She ignored him.

"Listen, I just wanted you to know… to see you one more time. Before I go." Joe caught a slight look of alarm ripple across Heather's reflected face. His heart started to thump.

"When are you going?"

"Early next week. We're nearly finished, way ahead of schedule. Just a couple of days more and, well, back to Hollywood, I guess."

Memories of the first night they kissed on the bridge filled Heather's thoughts as she looked away.

"Have a nice trip then, Mr Yates," she said as a hot tear stung the corner of her eye. Joe moved towards her.

"Heather."

"What?"

"That moody Irish female act doesn't suit you. You're no

Maureen O'Hara."

Heather turned to face Joe.

"And you're certainly no John Wayne either, Mr Joseph Yates."

Tears were now rolling down her face.

Joe slowly raised Heather's face so that she was now looking him in the eye.

"Heather, even John Wayne isn't John Wayne all the time, you know. Listen. There's something I want to say to you."

Joe slowly closed the gap between them, moving towards her as someone might delicately approach a small fawn in the middle of a forest.

"I've been doing a lot of thinking and, well, if you don't want to leave, and I love you, and I think you love me, and it doesn't seem to rain here as often as they say it does, and most people in these parts speak some kind of English… then I reckon it's not such a bad place to be. Even for a non-religious soon-to-be unemployed gofer like me. So. What do you say?"

At last, thought Heather, as she reached up and slowly stroked Joe's face.

"That's all I wanted to hear, Joe," she said softly. "That's all I ever really wanted to hear."

"Good!"

He threw his arms around her waist and lifted her from the ground. They kissed long and hard, their passion for each other reignited with an intensity neither could or wanted to control. Heather smothered him in kisses as Joe continued to hold her in the air.

"Listen" he gasped, fighting for air through her kisses. "Where are we going to live?"

Heather pulled away, a wicked glint in her eyes. Joe grimaced. "God, not with your parents?"

"Good grief, no. We're going to live in Cleveland."

Joe looked at her as if she had gone completely mad. He put her down on the ground, his confusion evaporating as the penny slowly dropped.

"You mean you'll come to the States?" said an incredulous Joe. "With me? Really?"

"Of course. I only wanted you to say you'd stay here with me so I'd know you truly loved me. As your John Wayne might say, it's an old trick but it might just work!"

"You little..."

Heather laughed as she wagged a cautionary finger in Joe's face.

"Joseph. Language." Joe held her again.

"Wait 'til you see America. Californian sunshine, there's nothing to beat it."

He saw the smile on Heather's face suddenly fade, and turned to see Michael Cassidy standing on the edge of the bridge with two of his ever-present cronies, Henry Molloy and Sean

Garrison.

Joe pushed Heather behind him as Cassidy grinned, doffing his hat and bowing to the couple on the bridge.

"Make way for the lovebirds, boys. A union made in heaven, if I may be so bold."

Joe slowly walked towards Cassidy as Heather whispered to him.

"For God's sake, Joe, let's run the other way. You don't have to fight him."

She gripped his arm for protection, as well as to stop him should he be tempted to strike out at Cassidy. Joe unhooked Heather's fingers, then put his face inches from Cassidy's.

"If you're looking for trouble I'm more than happy to accommodate you. But I suggest we pursue this matter at a time when the young lady is not present."

Cassidy doubled up with laughter as Molloy crept behind Joe and knelt on the ground. Before Heather could shout any warning Cassidy jumped up and pushed Joe backwards.

"Seems every time I see you you're always ending up flat on your arse," said Cassidy, clenching his fists in readiness.

As Joe disentangled himself from Molloy, Heather ran at Cassidy, shouting at the top of her voice as she swung her fist at him.

"Leave us alone you..."

Joe managed to get up from the ground in time to grab

Heather before her fist could make contact with Cassidy's head. Pulling her out of the way, Joe swung at Cassidy with all his might, catching him square on the jaw. Blood flowed from Cassidy's mouth as he fell pole-axed to the ground.

This time it was Joe's turn to stand over Cassidy, fists ready for action, but Garrison suddenly grabbed Joe's arms from behind as Cassidy stumbled to his feet. Molloy pushed Heather back against the wall of the bridge as her fists flailed at the air. Cassidy punched Joe in the stomach then socked him in the side of the head, Joe straining all the time to break Garrison's grip but to no avail. Cassidy and Garrison dragged Joe off the bridge and down the path towards the tree next to the stream where Ford had filmed Wayne punching the stunt man into the water only a couple of weeks before. Heather gave up trying to get past Molloy, turning to scream a warning at the other two boys.

"Michael Cassidy. Garrison. Take your hands off him or I'll kill the both of you, so help me I will!"

Ignoring Heather's shrill threats, Cassidy and Garrison dumped a struggling Joe into the cold water. Joe's efforts to pull himself from the stream distracted Molloy long enough for Heather to place a well-aimed kick between his legs.

As Molloy gasped for breath she ran over to Cassidy and jumped onto his back, scratching and clawing at his face and eyes. He screamed in pain and threw her off his back, but as she teetered on the edge of the bank Cassidy booted her into the river where she fell onto Joe, knocking him back into the water.

Cassidy, Garrison and a decidedly sick-looking Molloy ran off as Joe and Heather hauled each other up onto the riverbank. She cupped Joe's face in her hands, kissing him non-stop on his bruised flesh.

"Joe, Joe, are you alright?"

He smiled through the pain, wincing and shivering at the same time.

"I should get beat up more often," he grinned as Heather continued to shower him in kisses. "Don't stop."

She pulled him close then entwined her shivering body around his, watching Cassidy and the others as they ran off into the village with a look of fixed determination on her face.

Mary was outside in the garden hanging the washing when she heard the commotion of slamming doors and ran into the house.

"Heather?" she cried, knowing that Patrick and Thomas would probably not be home until the evening. She saw wet footprints leading from the front door and followed them up the stairs to Heather's bedroom. Mary opened the door to find her daughter struggling out of her wet blouse and skirt.

"Mother of God," gasped Mary. "What on earth have you

been up to?"

Heather grabbed a towel from the top of her wash basin and started to furiously dry her hair.

"Your Mr Cassidy," spat Heather.

"What do you mean, my Mr Cassidy?"

"You know who I mean. That idiotic little thug you regard so highly."

Heather sat on the bed in front of a small dressing table and started to brush her tangled hair, her wet slip soaking the top of the bedclothes. Mary surveyed Heather's reflection in the wooden framed mirror on the dresser.

"What did he do?"

"Him and two of his slimy friends threw me and Joe into the river down by the bridge."

"Since when have you started seeing Joe again?"

Heather turned to face her mother.

"That's just wonderful, mother. Thank you for your warmth and understanding. I get assaulted in broad daylight by three men twice my size, and all that concerns you is whose company I'm keeping."

Mary struggled to express herself in the face of Heather's indignation.

"Cassidy threw... but why? I don't understand."

Heather turned away as she continued to tug at her hair.

"I'm fed up to here with the small-minded petty gossip you

and your friends indulge in whenever it comes to matters that do not concern you. I am old enough to make up my own mind what I wish to do and with whom I wish to do it with. And I will not live in this insignificant, shabby little village any longer than is necessary."

Heather shook the brush at her mother.

"As soon as Joe leaves, I'm going with him. And that's an end to it."

Mary's features hardened as she moved further into the room, compelled by habit to confront her daughter.

"You listen to me, my..."

Their eyes met in the mirror. Heather's look of anger and resentment stopped Mary cold. Heather threw down the hair brush and walked around the bed towards her mother, the force of her words pushing Mary from the room a little at a time.

"No. It's too late for words, mother. I will not listen to you at all. In fact, I don't think I'm ever going to listen to anything you ever have to say to me again. Because you have nothing to say that interests me in the slightest. You've had your life, you had your chance, you drove our father away..."

Mary's hand flew to her chest in shock.

"Me?"

"Yes. You, mother, you. I see that now. I should have known it all along, but I was too blinded by my bitterness towards him to really understand what happened between you two. So don't stand there and try and tell me you know better than I do. As soon as I can I'm getting out of this place once and for all so don't waste your breath. I've made up my mind and that's all there is to it."

The two women found themselves standing inches apart and a million miles away from each other.

"Now, if it's alright with you I'd like to get dressed. I have to go back to work."

Mary slowly retreated from the bedroom. She walked downstairs weeping silently to herself, knowing from that moment onwards that things between her and Heather would never be the same. Her daughter had finally come of age and the young woman upstairs was now a complete stranger to her.

CHAPTER TEN

Thomas pestered his father all day about the electricity celebrations to be held in Ryan's Bar, making him promise on the Bible that he would not be left out of the festivities and stuck on the pavement outside the pub with a bottle of lemonade and a packet of soft crisps for company. He wanted to see John Wayne once more before the crew left the village, and so did his friends.

Patrick assured his son that he had spoken with Dunphy on this very matter, and arrangements had been made to accommodate a number of youngsters well away from the bar, but close enough to witness the proceedings whereby John Wayne would extinguish the last gas lamp in the village before Maureen O'Hara switched on the first electric light.

Thomas skipped off to play with Michael and Billy secure in the knowledge that his father had taken care of everything.

Joe and Heather made plans to meet at Ryan's later that evening, promising each other that soon they would be together in another place light year's from Cong. Joe told her that all she had to worry about was to sort out a passport and apply for her visa as quickly as possible. Heather in turn started to fret on what to wear on the flight, leaving Joe to secretly muse upon how he was going to break the news of his engagement to his highly strung mother.

Of course then he'd have to give some thought as to how he and Heather might support themselves financially. Maybe he'd get hired on the movie Ford planned to make next back in the States, but sucking up to the old man wasn't his style. Anyway, Ford despised yes men with a vengeance, even more than his refusal to suffer fools gladly. So Joe decided to trust in that old standby, fate. He would just take the cards that life dealt him. With Heather he knew he had a winning hand.

Despite wanting to get back to the States, finish *The Quiet Man* then move on to the next project, Ford started to feel ambivalent about leaving Cong. His Irish blood pulled him back to his roots, and he consoled himself with the fact that he would come back to Ireland as soon as possible to make another film. In the meantime he would channel the disappointment at not actually having been born Irish into his films instead.

John Wayne just wanted to buy everybody a drink.

Patrick stole a nip from Vincent's batch of newly-brewed poteen, countering the burning liquid that flowed through his body with a sharp intake of breath. Vincent emerged from behind the curtain that covered the doorway to the still room. He held a small glass of pure, clear poteen in his hand, a wide smile plastered across his ruined face. Patrick was still trying to bring his breathing under control, the poteen now settling like warm coals in the bed of his stomach.

"Is that some of the new stuff? Do you want I should give it a taste for quality, be a guinea pig, like?" offered Patrick helpfully.

Vincent ignored him as he held the glass up to the light in search of impurities.

"Crystal clear," marvelled Vincent, as if he had just discovered the meaning of life. "Absolutely crystal clear. No floaties in there. Beats Hanratty's mouse piss any day of the year."

Patrick looked at the clear liquid, totally unimpressed.

"Personally I can never tell the difference."

"When are you going to stop draining all my booze and get up off your arse? I thought we were paying Hanratty's a visit tonight? It's starting to get dark out already."

"All in good time. The festivities must be in full flow before we make our way into the enemy camp, so to speak."

Patrick helped himself to another swig of poteen.

"Yes, well, the festivities are certainly in full flow in the house of Corrigan, right enough," complained the old man as he attempted to prise the bottle out of Patrick's hands.

"When you've finished," said Vincent, with heavy sarcasm, "maybe you'll help me hitch the donkey up to the cart."

"What for?" asked a disinterested Patrick as he sampled the delights of Vincent's home made poison.

"I don't hear you volunteering to carry two barrels of beer back up from the village. How else are we supposed to get it back here?"

"Oh, aye, Vincent, that's right. Yes. Of course. I knew we'd be needing a horse and cart and everything. Don't you worry now, I've got it all planned out."

"Sure, and I'm the Pope," muttered Vincent beneath his breath before attending to matters of transport.

Making his way towards the room where Vincent kept his still, Patrick stuck his finger beneath the tap outlet and tasted some of the clear poteen his host had waved in front of his nose moments before.

"Hmmmm. A little more sugar, if I'm not mistaken."

He poked his head back through the curtain to make sure Vincent was still outside, then retrieved a two-pound bag of sugar from beneath the table and poured all of it into a funnel located at the top of the copper tubing. Crumpling up the bag Patrick stroked the boiler in the middle of the tubing affectionately.

"Don't go away now. I'll be back."

Patrick stood in the doorway watching Vincent as he harnessed his faithful donkey, Daisy, to an old wooden milk cart, the cart having weathered the years a damned sight better than the emaciated creature now attached to it.

"And where do you think you're going?" barked Vincent as

Patrick started to walk off down the road towards the village.

"I'm off to Ryan's to avail myself of some of that free booze floating around courtesy of Mr John Ford and his fine friends. It's all part of the plan, Vincent, trust me."

"I wouldn't trust you if you told me tomorrow was Monday," Vincent fumed. "And what am I supposed to be doing while you freeload off of that Hollywood lot?"

"Vincent. Don't you worry about a thing now. I'll meet you outside Hanratty's in about twenty minutes. And by the way, that donkey of yours is pissing on your foot."

Vincent shook his wet boot as Patrick headed off towards the village then turned to go back into the house to change his footwear, walking smack into Gerald O'Brien in the process.

"Jesus Christ, O'Brien, you scared the hell out of me," cried the old man, his hand automatically reaching across his chest to pat his heart. "What do you want?"

"I've come for me stuff."

"Stay there," warned Vincent, glad that the wretched dynamite was finally going to be removed from his house. Disappearing behind the still room curtain, Vincent knelt down and scrambled around on his arthritic knees beneath the table and retrieved O'Brien's two bundles of dynamite. The tape on one of the bundles had worked itself loose, and as he struggled to his feet one stick fell out and rolled back under the table.

Vincent contemplated whether or not he should get back down on his knees and find it. He decided he was too bloody old and O'Brien too bloody ungrateful and just left the stick of dynamite beneath the table. He'd pick it up another time.

He gave the bundles to O'Brien, holding his hand out for a reward of some kind, coinage or notes, he wasn't too bothered. Either way, Vincent desired a modicum of recognition for his contribution to the cause. Even though he had no idea what that cause might be. O'Brien ignored Vincent's outstretched hand as he checked the dynamite.

"There's a stick missing."

"Nothing much gets past you now, does it?" replied Vincent, heavy on the sarcasm.

O'Brien grabbed the old man by the collar. Vincent quickly looked around the room to see if there was a conveniently located object to brain O'Brien with.

"Listen to me, you old…"

He stopped and sniffed the air.

"What's that stink?"

Vincent raised his head and savoured the atmosphere as well.

"It's my new batch. I'm trying a different recipe."

O'Brien wrinkled his nose in disgust and let go of Vincent's collar.

"Smell's like horse piss to me."

Vincent shrugged, neither confirming or denying his willingness to experiment with exotic additives when searching for the perfect home-made elixir. O'Brien moved towards the door, waving the bundles of dynamite in Vincent's direction.

"I'll be back for the rest another time, old man. And remember, if word of this gets out to anybody they'll be dragging Lough Corrib for years before they find enough pieces to put you back together again."

As he turned and left the house Vincent administered the time-honoured two fingered salute to O'Brien, safe in the knowledge that the idiot was more of a danger to himself than he could ever be to the immediate community.

Heather was going through the sparse collection of clothes in her wardrobe, deciding what to wear for that evening, when she was disturbed by the unfamiliar sound of a timid knock on her door. "That can't be my mother," she thought to herself. "Her knock is always angry and loud. And it can't be Thomas either. He never knocks." A curious Heather swung open the door to reveal her mother standing outside. She turned away and continued carefully studying the contents of her wardrobe rather more intently than before as Mary entered the room and sat on the end of Heather's bed. The cold and icy silence between the both of them remained intact for a few moments until Mary finally spoke up.

"I knew somebody like you once." Heather continued to ignore her mother as she ran her hands down the lines of the same dress for the umpteenth time. Mary continued.

"Young. Impetuous. Frustrated. Impatient to leave this village and make a life of her own." Heather slowly started paying attention to what her mother was saying even though she not yet prepared to look at her.

"Then she met someone," said Mary. "Someone from the village. Before she knew it she was trapped." An intrigued Heather finally sat on the other end of the bed, a few feet away from her mother.

"Why was she trapped?" Heather asked, still not making eye-contact with her mother. Mary's voice descended to an almost inaudible whisper.

"Something happened to her, something that meant she would have to stay in the village forever."

"What happened to her?" asked Heather in equally soft tones. Mary took a deep breath and whispered even more quietly.

"You. You happened to her." Heather moved closer to her mother.

"Me?"

"You."

It took a moment or two before it dawned upon Heather what it was Mary was struggling to confess to her. Both women finally looked straight at each other.

"You mean –?" Mary nodded and smiled ruefully.

"It was the only honourable thing your father ever did. And even then I had to drag him out of the pub and down to the church." The silence descended between them again, a silence that had now lost the previous edge of antagonism that Heather had maintained at the beginning of their conversation.

"You were born seven months later. We told everyone you were premature – but they knew. Everyone in the village knew. No one ever said anything, not to my face anyway, but they knew. That's why I hate this place more than you'll ever know."

"Is that why – is this why you don't want me to see Joe?"

"What if he leaves you?" cried Mary. "What if –?" Heather moved towards her mother and embraced her.

"Oh mother." They both started to cry.

"Joe's not like that. I promise you. We've hardly held hands." Mary reached into her apron pocket and pulled out a small handkerchief.

"That's how it starts. Trust me." Heather borrowed the kerchief and dabbed at her eyes.

"Might have been worse, I suppose," she said.

"How?" asked Mary.

"It could have been Flanagan." They laughed and embraced

once more. Mary stroked Heather's cheek.

"You know, we're not that far apart in years. I used to fancy we could pass as sisters." "Fancy a night out, then?" asked Heather.

"Why not?" agreed Mary.

O'Brien moved quickly through the ever-increasing darkness towards his rendezvous with the poles of the ESB, determined to wreak his revenge upon those who sought to deprive him of… of what he wasn't sure if he were perfectly honest with himself. But matters had progressed to the point where there was now no turning back. His conscience was perfectly clear, having rationalised his actions a long time ago in the only way he knew how. He was doing it in the name of God. The Lord's will be done, O'Brien murmured to himself as he saw his target for tonight looming towards him in the late evening light. And if the Almighty needed a helping hand every now and then from a mere mortal such as O'Brien, so much the better. He crept over the wall next to the site from where he had stolen the dynamite. The place was deserted, the ESB people down in the village celebrating with all the other turncoats. Igniting a small petrol lamp left next to a corrugated iron hut O'Brien walked back up the road and selected the pole upon which he would bring down the wrath of God. He held one of the bundles up to the light to illuminate the instructions stencilled on the side of each stick, reading to himself.

"Place detonator in slot on top of dynamite."

He reached inside his jacket pocket. No detonators.

"Damn and blast!"

Running back to the site he scrambled around inside the hut, but to no avail. All the vehicles had long since gone as well, the site now deserted. He made his way back up the road to retrieve the dynamite, raising the lamp above him to take one last look at the wooden carrier of electricity that pointed skywards, contemptuous of an unforgiving God.

And then he saw them for the first time. Iron footholds either side of the pole, starting at eye-level then going all the way to the top. Digging deep inside his trouser pockets O'Brien found his trusty pen-knife, won many years ago in a rigged poker game. Placing the knife in his mouth and hooking the lamp on the first step O'Brien grabbed the foothold on the other side and jumped up onto the pole, hauling himself hand over hand towards the top, determined to finish the job.

Or die in the process.

Ryan's Bar was packed to the rafters. Half the population of County Mayo and the surrounding countryside had decided to drop in and celebrate along with the villagers and, of course, to meet the big Hollywood stars.

Wayne, Ford, Maureen O'Hara and the rest of the film crew mingled with the crowd, whilst Quinn's quartet played in the background, the musicians having placed themselves strategically next to the bar. Patrick entered the pub, momentarily struck by the thought as to why he had ever left such a friendly community in the first place. Even Mary looks happy, he said to himself, smiling to his wife before taking a seat next to her.

Joe and Heather had managed to get a couple of seats around a table near the entrance. Mary sat with them, nursing a small brandy and lemonade. Patrick kept his thought to himself, but he was expecting Mary to be quite upset at him, seeing as he had promised he would get Thomas and his friends into the pub somehow and indeed he had kept that promise, arranging with Dunphy for the young boys to sit in the snug that Joe and Heather had once shared.

Patrick leaned over the table and shouted to Joe above the din. "Joe, Joe, I was thinking. When you and Heather get to America, send me a newspaper so's I can see what kind of work they've got out there. Would you do that for me?"

Patrick caught Joe giving Heather a questioning look as Heather just shook her head emphatically.

Joe nodded, then looked to where Gene and Bo leaned against the bar, both of them watching a delighted Gallagher chatting animatedly to Maureen O'Hara.

Gene winked at Joe, laughing at the besotted ironmonger. Grinning, Gallagher took O'Hara's hand and placed a dainty kiss upon her fingers. The actress smiled politely then moved through the crowd to sit next to John Ford who occupied a place of honour in an easy chair next to the bar, sipping whisky from a large glass tumbler.

Dunphy stood behind the counter overseeing the hired barmen called in to help serve the thirsty crowd. He checked his watch then rang the bell usually reserved for last orders. The assembled throng duly paid attention.

"Thirty minutes to lighting up time," announced Dunphy, the crowd erupting into a loud cheer and surging towards the bar to slake their collective thirst.

O'Brien was with the gathering in the pub in spirit at least, wanting nothing more than to sink a pint or two as he swayed precariously over fifty feet from the ground. Sweat dripped down his back from the exertion of climbing the electricity pole.

He hung on with one hand, holding the lamp in the other with the knife still clenched between his teeth. He looked down at the ground but it was too dark and too far away to see, as though he were suspended above the middle of a bottomless pit. Just when he thought he might want to surrender to common sense and retire from his crusade, the wind carried the sound of the revellers in the village across the fields, taunting O'Brien into action.

Hooking the lamp onto one of the top rungs, he undid his belt with his free hand and for safety's sake strapped himself to the iron step located at waist level then looped his arm through the step at shoulder height. Taking the knife, he started to saw through the nearest wire.

Within an instant O'Brien and the twentieth century finally collided head-on approximately fifty feet above ground level. The blade quickly sliced through the insulation then made contact with the inner live wire. The voltage shot through the knife, up his arm, across every single nerve ending in his body then exploded at the base of his skull.

The force of the shock sent him soaring out into the dark night, his belt pulling him with a bone-crunching thud back against the pole and knocking O'Brien into welcome unconsciousness. The lamp, still balanced miraculously at the top of the pole, bathed O'Brien's rear end in yellow light as he swayed in the breeze, whilst the sound of cheering from the village echoed through the night.

Back in Ryan's Bar the celebrations started to take on a sense of urgency as the time neared to turn off the last gas lamp and switch on the electricity. Thomas and his friends peered happily around the corner of the snug watching the villagers descend further into a united state of inebriation.

"You see, Joseph," said Patrick with one eye on the clock, as he continued to play the dutiful father, "Under normal circumstances I wouldn't be letting my little girl wander off with the first feller that comes along now, you get my meaning? She deserves better than that, I think you'd agree."

Joe's reply was forceful, in order to be heard above the din.

"I certainly do, Mr O'Dea. But with all due respect Heather's old enough to make up her own mind about what she wants to do. And what with you not being around all that much, she's had a lot of responsibility placed on her shoulders. So I guess she should be pretty well placed to knows what she's doing."

He had been as diplomatic as he possibly could, but his patience was already starting to wear thin with Patrick. It was bad enough trying to get Heather away from the mother, Joe was damned if he was going to spend too much time trying to wrest her from a man who'd disappeared and left his family in the lurch for two years.

Patrick took another look at the clock above the bar.

"True, Joseph, true. I've not exactly been a model father, I'll give you that."

Patrick's contriteness failed to impress Joe. Just as he was about to reply he felt Heather moving next to him as she leaned across to listen in on the conversation.

Patrick gave his daughter a quick smile.

"Joseph. I have to ask you. What are your intentions?"

At this point an interested Mary leaned across the table as well. Joe started his case for the defence.

"Well, Mr O'Dea, first of all I'd like Heather to come over to America as soon as her visa comes through, meet my folks and, if she still feels the same way about me as she does now, we'll come back here and get married. In Cong."

The couple glanced lovingly at each, Joe wanting to be somewhere else with Heather at that moment rather than stuck in the middle of Ryan's Bar, surrounded on both sides by her parents.

"Separate bedrooms I take it?"

"Patrick!"

Mary crossed herself and glared at her husband.

Joe figured he hadn't heard correctly.

"I'm sorry? Separate what?"

"I'm meaning that if Heather is to join you in America, I assume you both plan to sleep in separate accommodation." Patrick returned Heather's glare with one of parental reproof.

"After all, I am her father, Joe. I'm entitled to an answer."

Joe could feel Heather's body trembling with anger.

"But of course, Mr O'Dea. I wouldn't have it any other way."

"Good," said Patrick with a nod. "Just checking."

Joe turned to Heather and smiled, only to catch a fleeting look of what appeared to be mild disappointment at the proposed sleeping arrangements. Patrick clapped his hands.

"Right. Now that's all out of the way, how's about a drink to honour the happy couple?"

He felt in his pockets one at a time.

"Oh, no. I've gone and left me wallet back at the house, would you believe it?"

"I would." said Heather. "You know what they say. 'The one who opens his mouth the most is he who opens his purse the least.' What'll it be?" she asked, retrieving some money from her bag.

Patrick reached across and grabbed Heather's wrist.

"Now you just wait, young lady, this one's on me. I'm going home to get my wallet and I'll be back here in no time to buy you's all a drink and that's all there is to it."

Patrick hot-footed it over to Hanratty's where a fuming Vincent Corrigan waited for him in the shadows by the side of the pub.

"There's a light on in the bar. I thought you said they'd all be over at Ryan's?"

"I could have sworn I saw both of them back at the bar," lied Patrick, having seen Sean Hanratty freeloading for all he was worth, but without the company of his elder brother Peter. "Tell you what, you go inside and check it out while I stay here and look after the donkey."

"No you bloody well don't. You're coming with me. This was your idea, not mine. If it weren't for you I could be over at Ryan's right now drinking me fill of cheap booze."

Not with Dunphy's boot up your miserable arse, thought Patrick as Vincent pushed him towards Hanratty's. They opened the door slowly and tip-toed quietly into the pub.

Back at Vincent's house, the extra bag of sugar added to the brew by an over-zealous Patrick had caused the mixture to boil over prematurely. The still was glowing red hot as the contraption of tubes and steel rods struggled to contain the large amount of steam emanating from within.

As usual, Hanratty's was totally deserted. Apart, that is, from the ever-diligent Peter, sat propped up on his stool with his back against the wall, arms folded for balance and sleeping the sleep of the dead.

"I should have known he'd be here," whispered Vincent. "He'd rather stand a round of drinks than enter Ryan's Bar, free or not."

The men moved closer to the sleeping figure.

"He has the key to the cellar on a piece of string around his neck," said Vincent, hinting that maybe Patrick should chance his arm and retrieve it by heftily pushing his partner in crime between the shoulder blades.

A tearful, drunken Gallagher nursed his drink as he leaned against Gene, interspersing his words with the occasional laughing sob as he regaled his new-found friend on the near-religious experience of finally having encountered Maureen O'Hara.

"She let me kiss her hand, Gene. Did you see?"

Gene nodded, having indeed witnessed the momentous occasion, and now found himself forced to listen to the story for the umpteenth time.

"She let me hold her dainty little fingers in mine so's I could kiss them, she did. She's a beauty, a real beauty."

Gene clapped his inebriated friend on the shoulder and bellowed above the noise.

"Well, at least you got to meet her face-to-face. That's something, I guess."

"It is, Gene, it is and I'll be forever grateful to you, on that you can be sure. And I'll tell you something else, too."

Gene leaned in closer.

"I'd marry her tomorrow if my heart wasn't betrothed to another, I would really."

"I thought Miss O'Hara was the only one for you, Mr Gallagher?"

Gallagher flapped his hand over his heart.

"Not any more. It's reserved for Miss Lorna Curtis. And before the night's out I'll be proposing marriage. Or my name's not Dermot Joseph Edward Aloycius Gallagher."

"Jeeze," mumbled Gene into his glass as he thought of all the trouble he'd gone to persuading Maureen O'Hara to seek out Gallagher personally. "There's no pleasing some people."

The bell rang out once more as Dunphy continued the countdown.

"Five minutes to go!"

The thin copper skin of the still glowed a dark red, the table upon which it rested shuddering and scraping across the floor as if to shake off the metal and glass beast that rode its back.

Late at night as he diligently cycled the mean roads of County Mayo, PC Flanagan would ponder why he had been chosen out of all his other colleagues back in Galway to take up his duties in this God-forsaken bogland. He'd made up his mind months ago to seek a transfer to somewhere a bit more livelier – in terms of lawlessness that is – than Cong. Two sheep rustlers, a chicken thief and assorted drunken offences did not exactly test Flanagan's eagerness when it came to the apprehension of criminals, this being the total sum of collars felt since being posted to the Garda station in Cong further back than he cared to remember.

Even the arrival of the film crew did nothing to raise the level of crime in and around the village, much to Flanagan's chagrin, downhearted that he hadn't been able to nab at least one of them Yanks up to a bit of no good in the last few weeks. Tonight, however, fortune smiled upon the disillusioned police constable, his much derided diligence about to be paid off in spades.

Resting his bicycle against one of the brand new electricity poles Flanagan shone his torch up into the by now semi-conscious face of self appointed freedom fighter and all-round scourge of the ESB, one Gerald Michael Collins O'Brien.

Vincent Corrigan and Patrick O'Dea slowly struggled to the top of the ramp leading up from the cellar behind Hanratty's, pushing a large barrel in front of them then letting it roll across the ground of its own volition before coming up
hard against the wooden cart. Groaning and sweating with the exertion of it all both men then heaved the barrel up onto the back of the small wagon.

Vincent's efforts were more vocal than physical.

"Come on, O'Dea, push now, push."

Patrick collapsed exhausted across the top of the barrel as he finally slid it into place.

"Well done, Patrick. Now, just one more then we'll be on our way."

Patrick wiped the sweat from his face as he fought for breath. "No," he gasped. "No more. Not tonight. I'm finished. I've got to be getting back to Ryan's otherwise they'll be missing me."

Vincent pointed with a shaking hand to the open cellar door.

"But there's a barrel of Guinness down there just waiting to be had."

"Don't be stupid. You know that stuff doesn't travel very well."

"You can't leave now, it's just there, waiting for us to take it, begging to be lifted"

"I said no more, old man, and I mean it," Patrick barked, his tone indicating there was nothing more to discuss on the matter. "Now. Let's get this back to your place then I'm off to Ryan's for a proper drink. None of that rotgut you've been pouring down me throat all evening."

A scowling Vincent climbed onto the cart while a tired and emotional Patrick began to doze off, the old man muttering dark thoughts to himself as he yanked the donkey's bridle.

Heather turned at the sound of Dunphy quietening the humming throng with a clattering ring of the bell, banging the bar at the same time to enforce the silence such an occasion deserved.

"If you please, ladies and gentlemen, Mr Dermot Gallagher would like to say a few words before the ceremony begins."

A cheer rang out from the crowd as an unsteady Gallagher made his way over to the bar. An initial attempt to perch on a stool met with failure, prompting Wayne and McLaglen to pick Gallagher up and seat him upon the counter.

Gallagher thanked the actors for their gesture, then raised his glass, all the while blinking his eyes back into focus as he swayed gently from side to side. Under normal circumstances this would have provoked much laughter, but seeing as most of the other people in the bar were also of a mind to sway in a similar manner, Gallagher's inebriated movements were not deemed to be out of the ordinary. To Heather, however, this was the first time she had seen Gallagher with a drink in his hand all the time she had known him, and the sight of her boss in a state of slight drunkenness came as a bit of a shock to her.

"Before our illustrious guest's usher in the beginning of a new dawn for this wonderful community of ours I'd just like to remind you all that Gallagher's Ironmongery will be open first thing tomorrow morning for the forward-thinking amongst us who wish to purchase the very latest in electrical appliances and assorted gadgets of the plug and socket variety. So now, without further ado...."

Gallagher cast a glance behind him at Dunphy to check everything was ready for the off.

"Mr John Wayne will very kindly dim the last gas lamp in

Ryan's Bar here, then the lovely Miss Maureen O'Hara will do us the honour of throwing the switch to turn on these glass contraptions hanging from the ceiling up there."

To the sound of much whistling and clapping, all the gas lamps in the pub were turned off, before Wayne reached across and turned down the wick on the lamp placed at the end of the bar.

The place was plunged into darkness.

The next second Maureen O'Hara threw a small switch fixed to the wall at the other end of the bar. As the ceiling lights flickered on, a loud cheer erupted from the crowd. A cheer that was instantly dashed as the lights went out, throwing Ryan's into pitch blackness once again.

Booing and moans of disappointment filled the room as Wayne reignited the gas lamp. John Ford pushed himself up from his chair and banged his glass on the bar for quiet, taking charge of the situation.

"Gene, Bo, you and Mr. Yates there go get the generator van. Let's see if we can't hook something up here for the people."

Joe blew Heather a kiss then left the pub with his friends to shouts of general encouragement and good cheer, while Ford took advantage of the distraction and poured himself a drink from Wayne's glass.

Flanagan pulled a limping and still heavily shocked O'Brien by the scruff of the neck up the steps of the Garda station. Small wisps of smoke trailed behind O'Brien and drifted off into the night air as he staggered into the building. He was still too stupefied to comprehend where he was or how he got to wherever he now happened to be. Flanagan pulled him through the front door of the station and down the stairs to the small holding cell in the basement of the building, frantically waving his hand in front of his nose to dispel the odorous combination of singed skin and the innate body odour of the unwashed. Holding O'Brien by the scruff of the neck with one hand and deftly juggling with his keys in the other, Flanagan deposited his stunned prisoner into the warm embrace of an empty cell. Slamming the door shut, he started for the stairs before stopping and looking back at a forlorn O'Brien.

"Now don't you go away, Gerald. And don't look so sad. Something tells me you won't be alone in that cell for very much longer."

Flanagan stood on the steps of the station grinning from ear to ear, highly pleased with himself. A small lamp above the door gave him just enough light to be able to roll a cigarette, one of his only vices. Still laughing to himself, he put the cigarette to his lips and was just about to light it when he heard the sound of hooves echoing slowly down the dark street to his left.

Furious clouds of steam filled Vincent's still room as the apparatus jumped across the table and teetered on the edge, flames now bursting from the top of the contraption.

The generator van had been left at the bottom of the main village street in anticipation of the following day's shoot. Joe gunned the engine and drove it the few hundred yards across to Ryan's Bar, parking it head-on to the pub with the lights on. He stayed in the cab while Gene, Bo and a few other volunteers from the film crew took a large cable from inside the back of the van then laid it out on the ground, below a junction box fixed to the wall. Bo reached up and took off the front of the box, studying the wiring by the lights of the generator van.

"Well?" said Gene.

"No problem," replied Bo.

He reached inside his pocket and pulled out a pair of wire clippers, cutting the main supply to the building. Quickly and silently Bo disappeared into the back of the van and came back with a large roll of insulating tape and a bar of electric plug sockets. Joe and the crew watched in silent admiration as Bo twisted, joined, cut, spliced and generally worked wonders in a matter of moments, the silence broken only by the sound of his harsh breathing as he concentrated on the task in hand. Running a set of wires from the junction box into the socket bar Bo then nodded to Joe.

"Okay. Turn it over."

Joe switched on the engine as Gene stuck his head around the door of the pub and called out to Ford.

"Okay, Pappy. Give it a go."

The crew ran in as Ford stood and bowed ceremoniously to Maureen O'Hara, waving his handkerchief like a little flag.

"Shine some light on the proceedings if you will, Miss O'Hara."

Wayne waited until all the other lamps had been extinguished before once more turning down the last lamp next to him. The actress then hit the switch, setting the whole room ablaze with light. The crowd waited in anticipation to see whether or not the lights would go off again, then the whole place burst into a cacophony of cheering and whistling as everybody realised the power was here to stay.

Wayne, Ford, O'Hara and McLaglen bowed and took in the applause as Joe and the rest of the crew entered the pub. Heather ran over and kissed Joe on the cheek. Mary looked on at Heather's public show of affection, hoping against hope that her daughter hadn't made a terrible mistake by falling for the young boy from America.

A curious PC Flanagan sat at the bottom of the station steps and took in the scene, now lit up like a frozen tableau before him. He could hardly contain himself at the sight of Vincent and Patrick in a cart containing a large barrel with the words *Property of Murphy's Brewery* stencilled on the side. A few more nights like this and his passport back to Galway, Dublin even, would be guaranteed.

At this point the still finally gave up the battle with gravity, steam and fire spitting in all directions as it fell screaming to the floor like a banshee from hell and made inevitable contact with Gerald O'Brien's rogue stick of dynamite.

Flanagan, Vincent and Patrick turned in unison in the direction of the explosion.
"Isn't that where your house is?" asked Patrick.
Wailing to the heavens, the old man shot off so fast towards his wrecked house not even the surprised and usually fleet-footed constable with the aid of a prevailing wind could have caught up with him.
Patrick jumped down from the cart in an effort to take advantage of Flanagan's distracted state of mind, but the officer was too quick for him, tripping Patrick up then handcuffing him to one of the railings outside the station before chasing off down the road after Vincent Corrigan.

Catching up with Vincent within seconds, Flanagan dragged him back down the street and sat him down on the steps of the station, the old man blaspheming himself into the record books as Patrick struggled with the handcuffs. Flanagan pointed threateningly at Vincent.

"Stay there, old man," warned Flanagan. "You try and run away and I may start to lose my temper". He then turned his attention to Patrick, handcuffing the both of them together then pulling the prisoners up the steps of the Garda station. Patrick stopped and took another look at the glowing sky above Vincent's former house then contemplated the brightly lit street before him.

"You know, for a minute there," said a wistful Patrick, "what with all those lights and everything, I could have sworn I was in Heaven."

Flanagan tugged him through the door.

"Oh no, you're definitely in Hell. Take my word for it."

CHAPTER ELEVEN

As usual Joe, Gene, Bo and practically every member of the cast and crew spent the following morning wishing they were six feet under. Apart that is from Ford, Wayne and McLaglen, all three past masters at waking up in the morning and seeing off anything their battered livers could throw at them.

Gene sat half-collapsed at the breakfast table and tried not to swivel his head more than five degrees in either direction for fear of falling off the chair, knowing full well that his compatriots were equally at sea as the alcohol rebuffed all efforts to flush the poison from their systems.

Ford surveyed his fallen warriors from the end of the table then rapped the surface with his pipe, eliciting a chorus of groans and the occasional pleas for mercy.

"Okay. Listen up. This is our last day. Let's make it a good one."

"Christ, how does he do it?" complained Gene loudly. Ford stood and drained his cup of coffee.

"When it comes to drinking whisky, Mr Willis, remember this" said Ford, banging the cup on the table for good measure. "It's the first drop that destroys you. There's no harm at all in the last. Now, I'm off to shoot the last scene of this movie. Anyone care to join me?"

Ford marched out of the dining room. It was at least another minute or two before the room echoed to the sound of chair l legs scraping across the floor as one by one the crew slowly pushed themselves to their feet like a dispirited army girding itself for the final attack.

"Remind me never to work with that son-of-a-bitch again," Bo said to no one in particular.

"You know, I'd kill myself if it wasn't for the fact that I'm supposed to be getting married soon," said Joe thickly, emitting his first words of the day.

Gene rose from the table.

"I'd wait until you've been married a few years before contemplating suicide.

I did."

"You still look very much alive to me."

"Speak for yourself."

Barry Fitzgerald sat atop the seat of his courting carriage while the make-up people powdered Mildred Natwick's nose. The actress, who played the widow Tillane and object of Victor McLaglen's affections, climbed onto the back of the carriage with the help of McLaglen. The three of them then sat in the late morning sun waiting for the lighting crew to finish setting up the equipment to shoot the last exterior scene before everybody packed up and left Cong for good.

The night before Joe had promised Heather that he would come and find her at Gallagher's to say goodbye before he left with the rest of the crew for Shannon Airport and home. As he stood in his usual place behind the camera, the assistant director called for quiet on the set for the last scene. Fitzgerald took up the reins and waited for Ford to call action.

Just before the camera rolled Joe caught sight of Thomas out of the corner of his eye, the young boy leaning against the wall with his arms folded, looking miserable. Joe went over and put his hand on Thomas's shoulder.

"This is the very last shot in the film. You see, McLaglen up there is courting the lady next to him and Fitzgerald plays chaperon to them."

Thomas showed not the slightest bit of interest, his head bowed low as he scuffed the pavement with his shoe. Joe leaned down further and saw that Thomas was crying.

Joe knelt down and gently ruffled the boy's hair.

"Don't look so sad, Thomas. I'll take care of your sister, I promise."

"It's not Heather I'm worried about," mumbled Thomas, the tears coursing down his face.

"What is it then? What's the problem?"

"It's my da. He said you were the only one who could help him."

Jack Boone flew out of Gallagher's Ironmongery as fast as his feet could carry him.

"I didn't know! I didn't know!" protested Boone, slamming the door so hard behind him that the window frame collapsed, showering an enraged Gallagher in broken glass and splintered wood. Despite his rotund figure Gallagher was surprisingly light on his feet, jumping nimbly through the broken door and waving a large electric iron and coil above his head as he chased his ex-business partner out of the village.

"All this stuff is wired up for the wrong voltage," Gallagher screamed. "I want me money back, do you hear me? I want me money back!", a sentiment that was forcefully and most loudly endorsed by the large crowd of people who had formed a rather disorderly queue outside Gallagher's to return their defective purchases.

Heather stepped lightly out of the shop over the broken glass and wood and watched with the other villagers as Gallagher ran off into the distance, the now bankrupted shop-keeper describing to Boone in quite explicit detail exactly where he was going to plug the faulty electrical appliances once he got his hands on him. Minnie Gallagher stood at the head of the queue, clutching a useless toaster under her arm and shaking her head in disgust at her son's vocal outpourings.

"If I were dead I'd spin in me grave and that's a fact."

She turned to Heather.

"It's a wonder you'd want to work here anymore after hearing shameful language such as that."

Heather bit her lip, knowing it would be her last day at Gallagher's very soon.

"Oh, don't you worry, Mrs Gallagher, I'll tell him a thing or two. If he ever comes back, that is."

Although she felt sorry for her employer and his somewhat shaky future as Cong's chief of commerce, Heather had more important matters to occupy her mind.

A convoy of lorries and trucks laden with equipment and assorted film crew members rumbled around the corner, then drove down the street and out of the village on their way towards Shannon airport. The villagers waved cheery goodbyes as the last truck pulled up outside the shop. Gene sat at the wheel with Bo in the middle seat as Joe jumped down from the cab.

"Write me the minute your visa comes through," said a breathless Joe. "I'll be waiting."

They hugged each other, both of them oblivious to the long queue of onlookers who had now turned their attention away from Gallagher towards the couple in the street. Gene hit the horn on the lorry to hurry his friend along.

"You'll meet me at the airport? In Cleveland?" she asked as Joe jumped onto the running board of the lorry.

"Don't you worry. Write me once you're booked on the flight.

I'll be there. I promise."

"Wild horses wouldn't keep me here," a delirious Heather assured him. "Don't forget to ask your mother to make up the spare bed."

Joe jumped back off the lorry and gave Heather one last hug to the accompaniment of the cheering villagers and Gene and Bo's cat-calling.

"Oh, by the way," said a smiling Joe. "Thomas told me about your father. He was really upset."

"My father's been nothing but trouble since he came back. At least if he's in gaol mother will know where he is, and I won't have to worry about her anymore. I can leave with a clear conscience."

Gene hit the horn once more.

"Hey, Joe, jump on. You two are gonna have plenty of time to canoodle later on. Let's go."

Joe grabbed the door handle and called to Heather as he pulled himself into the cab.

"I gave Thomas some money. He said he needed to bail your father out. Give him my regards."

Joe waved cheerfully as the truck drove off. Heather went rigid with shock, the colour draining from her face as everything she had dreamed and prayed for was cruelly snatched from her grasp in a second.

"Oh no, Joe," she whispered. "What have you done? What

have you done?"

Mary rocked in her chair, clutching a broken-hearted Thomas to her breast when Heather burst through the front door.
"Where is he?" she asked, knowing the answer already but clinging to one last hope that it might all be a terrible misunderstanding. But her mother's tears told a different story. Mary silently indicated the note next to the clock on the mantelpiece. Heather took it down and read aloud:

"I'm sorry to have been such a burden but I'll be back once I have enough to pay my way. Tell Thomas he's the best boy a father could want. Ask Heather to forgive me. Patrick."

Heather folded the piece of paper and placed it in the drawer of a small table in the corner of the parlour.
"You know father," she said, disbelieving everything she said even as the words tumbled from her mouth. "He'll be back, I'm sure of it."
"But when?" cried Mary. "What am I going to do with your father not here and you off to America with Joe? What will become of me and Thomas?"
"But Joe and I, we're... we were..."
She turned away, clenching her fists in frustration as she tried to hold on to her composure, the sudden tears burning her

face. She blinked and looked at her mother. It struck her how much Mary had aged in the last few weeks, how much closer to sixty she looked instead of a woman of thirty-nine. Heather didn't know if it was the sudden departure of her father that had so drastically affected Mary's appearance, or if she were truly seeing her mother for the first time. A woman beaten and brought to her knees by an irresponsible husband and the harsh reality of having to raise two children in circumstances not of her own making.

"Don't worry, mother," Heather said softly. "I'm not going anywhere. Not until father comes back. I promise."

Mary stood with her arm around Thomas and held her daughter close, the three of them weeping for a man they found so hard to hate and all too easy to love.

Mary wiped the tears from her face.

"I'm sorry, Heather. You must think I'm so pathetic but I don't know what I'd do without you, really I wouldn't."

Heather tenderly stroked her mother's hair then ran for the door.

"I'll be back in a minute. I have to catch up with Joe."

"Not without me," said Thomas, jumping up from his mother's lap and following his sister out of the house.

Heather and Thomas ran up the main street then down past Gallagher's and on out of the village until they reached the top of a hill overlooking the road leading out of Cong. The convoy of lorries and trucks snaked off into the distance past Lough Corrib towards the hills of Connemara, too far away by now for either Thomas or Heather to catch them. Heather waved goodbye to the fast-disappearing vehicles, knowing Joe would come back for her one day, the certainty of his returning causing her to almost burst with happiness until she was laughing and crying at the same time.

Feeling a sudden tug on her sleeve, Heather turned and saw Thomas waving to a figure in the distance.

"It's da", said Thomas. They both watched as Patrick crested the brow of the hill then vanished from sight. Heather felt Thomas squeeze her hand.

"Don't cry, Heather. He'll come back, I'm sure of it."

Heather brushed the hair from her face as the warm breeze blew in from across the Lough and pulled her brother close.

"I know he will, Thomas. One day. One day."

The last truck finally disappeared from view over the hills far away. Heather and Thomas turned and walked back to Cong hand in hand, back to their mother. Back to their home.

EPILOGUE
1992

It struck Thomas how little the village had really changed since 1951. Rose Cottage still bloomed like a giant flower on the bridge where he stood with Heather and Joe. The three of them were silent for a few moments, lost in their own thoughts. Thomas eventually broke the stillness.

"It's good they're buried side by side. At least mother's going to know where father is from now on." Heather tried to suppress a snigger and failed. Thomas leaned over the wall of the bridge and breathed in the clean sweet air rising from the stream below.

"Ah, the smell of Cong. Nothing like it. Clean, fresh and invigorating."

"Wish you'd stayed?" asked Joe.

"Good God no", replied Thomas emphatically. "I'd have gone stark raving mad spending the rest of my life here. But it's a good place to come home to." He checked his watch then turned to Heather with an apologetic grin.

"I know this isn't very polite but I've really got to get back to Dublin and catch the plane otherwise I'm going to miss the connection." Heather nodded understandingly and kissed him on the cheek. Joe reached across and shook his brother-in-law's hand.

"You know, Joe, I'm not sure I ever thanked you properly," said Thomas.

"For what?"

"For coming back to Cong all those years ago. If it hadn't been for you I'm not sure I'd have been able to leave. I owe you more than I can ever repay."

"My pleasure, Tom," replied Joe cheerfully. "Just try and get back here more often. You never know, you might get to like it here."

"Why not?" said Thomas as he hugged Heather once more before walking from the bridge. "After all, you did."

He turned and waved one last time before heading back to the car. Heather and Joe held each other as they stood on the bridge where they had kissed for the first time all those years ago. She looked up at her husband, momentarily glimpsing the young Joe Yates she had fallen in love with so many years before.

"I've got an idea," said Heather as she took Joe's arm. "Why don't we take the long way home?"

"I thought you'd never ask." Said Joe.

THE END

AUTHOR'S NOTE

Connemara Days is a work of fiction and is a revised version of the book I self-published back in 1999. The book is based upon a screenplay written a few years before for a film that has yet to be produced, although with a fair wind that day may yet still come. As far as I am aware no one called Joe Yates or Gene Willis or Bo Willard worked as crew members on 'The Quiet Man'. All the characters apart from the real life actors and crew on the film are figments of my imagination and bear absolutely no resemblance to anyone who lived in Cong in 1951.

I want to extend my thanks to the late lamented Tom Ryan who proof read the original manuscript for the first version of this book and suggested a number of changes to ensure there was nothing to offend. As for the newly revised version of Connemara Days I must thank professional proof reader Sarah Palmer for turning my original efforts into a more concise and readable book.

I must also mention Michael Langdon who provided the wonderful cover art, Brian Sweet who set up the mostlywesterns.com website that enabled me to reach out to literally thousands of like-minded John Wayne fans, and Mark Stay of the Orion Publishing Group who provided much-needed help and guidance on navigating my way through the uncharted waters – for me anyway – of online publishing.

Finally, a special mention for the late Hollywood film director Andrew V. McLaglen who, back in the late 1990s, took the time to share his memories with me on working with John Ford, John Wayne, Maureen O Hara and his father Victor on 'The Quiet Man'.

Made in the USA
Coppell, TX
21 December 2019